HOOP CITY

CHICAGO

SAM MOUSSAVI

EPIC
Press

Chicago
Hoop City: Book #3

Written by Sam Moussavi

Copyright © 2016 by Abdo Consulting Group, Inc.

Published by EPIC Press™
PO Box 398166
Minneapolis, MN 55439

Cover design by Nicole Ramsay
Images for cover art obtained from Shutterstock.com
Edited by Lisa Owens

LIBRARY OF CONGRESS CATALOGING-IN-PUBLICATION DATA

Moussavi, Sam.
Chicago / Sam Moussavi.
p. cm. — (Hoop city)
Summary: When Serge is recruited from the Sudan to come play basketball at a
high profile prep school in Chicago, there are bigger obstacles than culture shock to
contend with. Will Serge be able to put his past behind him and make something of
his life in America through basketball?
ISBN 978-1-68076-044-6 (hardcover)
1. Basketball—Fiction. 2. High schools—Fiction. 3. Inner cities—Fiction.
4. Teamwork—Fiction. 5. Young adult fiction. I. Title.
[Fic]—dc23
2015903973

EPIC
Press

EPICPRESS.COM

*To Marina, with a white butterfly fluttering
just above her shoulder*

ONE

I woke up suddenly with cold sweat beaded on my forehead. A sour smell of death filled the room and it felt like the air was sucked from my body. I could hear the sound of their voices in the night—shouting, not speaking—forceful and demanding. Their voices were bold because of the guns they held in their hands. Who knows how strong they would have been without them?

I could hear the sound of their voices in the night. The next sound I heard was the shots.

Then I woke up.

It was just a dream.

The dream came to me less and less, but I never

knew when it would come back again. The fear of it paralyzed me.

———

Until the age of thirteen, basketball was a distant and foreign thing to me. I couldn't call playing the game a "dream" because I didn't even know what the sport was until then. When I saw it played for the time, though—the game with the round, orange ball—I fell in love instantly. There was something mesmerizing about the players running up and down the floor, jumping into the air to block shots and grab rebounds, and the odd act of throwing a ball into a hole for points. It looked like freedom. I didn't understand what it meant to be free until I stepped onto the court for the first time. I had no concerns while I was on the court and time seemed to stand still. I just played.

Players used their strengths and covered their

weaknesses the best they could just so they could stay on the court. I wanted to know. I wanted to understand what my strengths and weaknesses were. But most of all, it was the competition that got me. I began playing every day soon after. Little by little, I got better.

I was born and raised in a small village in the south of Sudan in a region called Darfur. It is a place where dreams do not exist. I quit school at the age of ten to help my father make money for the family. My father was a sugarcane farmer and every morning at five, he, my older brother Sefu, and I, would wake up and walk five miles to the plantation.

He was a good man, my father. He was a man who loved and protected his family until the very end of his life. He didn't have much, but always gave what he had to us. Sefu was the same as my father. The responsibility of helping the family was a serious matter to him and he tried to pass that sense of responsibility down to me as well.

My parents had six children. Three of us were boys: Sefu, my younger brother—Denji—who wasn't old enough to work yet, and me. My older sister, Maya, helped my mother with housework and caring for my two younger sisters, Fazilah and Talia.

During the first few years, I didn't mind going to work with my father and Sefu because it was the only thing I knew. And besides, school wasn't a necessity in Sudan like it is in America. When basketball came into my life, though, working on the plantation became harder for me. Even though I was in the fields working, my mind was elsewhere. I dreamt of being on the basketball court, of soaring through the air on the way to a dunk or a blocked shot. I never said anything about it, though—this dream of mine. I never complained about being in the fields, and I never said a cross word to my father or Sefu. The three of us rarely talked on the walks to and from the plantation, in fact. My father was a man of few words—a trait he passed down to my older brother and me.

I worked on the sugarcane plantation until the age of fifteen. That was when basketball became a possible way out of Sudan.

TWO

There I was at the airport in Khartoum, during the fall of my sixteenth year, ready to fly to America. I had never seen a plane before, let alone set foot on one. Chicago, Illinois, was to be my new home. I knew as much about it as I did about any other American city—next to nothing. My feelings were mixed as I waited in the terminal for the first "leg" of my voyage—a connecting flight to Nairobi. I watched with excitement as the airplanes took off and soared into the air. The places the passengers were going didn't matter; the point was that we were leaving Sudan. There was also a sense of personal excitement knowing that I was going some place new and leaving behind a place of sadness. I was also sad to be leaving my family behind in that place. I didn't know if leaving them behind was the right thing to do.

It wasn't until a month earlier—when my mother gave me her blessing—that I made the decision to leave Sudan with a clear heart. She told me that it was my duty to go to America to play basketball. It was my duty to make a better life for myself, either through education or the game. Her hope was that in the process, maybe I could make my family's life better as well. The last thing my mother told me before I left for the airport was that if my dad and Sefu were still alive, they would have wanted me to go, too. I wasn't so sure about that, but I smiled and hugged my mother goodbye. I could feel the warmth in her body. I quickly realized that I wouldn't feel warmth like that again for a long time, if ever again.

Reality set in when I got onto the plane. I looked out of the window and clutched my old, tattered copy of *The Jungle Book*. It was one of the few possessions that I brought with me. I said silent goodbyes to my family as I stared out to the nothingness surrounding the airport. I thought about my life in Sudan. It wasn't all bad, but my thoughts rested on the painful memory of my father and Sefu. I decided to stop thinking just then, to instead look forward and be thankful.

The connecting legs of my voyage were exhausting—a three-hour wait in Nairobi, another four-hour stop, two hours of delay in Amsterdam, and finally a three-hour layover in Boston, Massachusetts, before finally moving on to Chicago. I arrived there—sore from squeezing my tall frame into the tight spaces of the airplanes—after thirty-six hours of traveling from Khartoum.

I stood outside the airport in this new place, waiting for a stranger to pick me up and take me to my new life. I didn't have a name or a clue as to who this person would be. I just knew he or she would be there when I landed.

Outside the airport, many people from all different parts of the world were hugging loved ones before loading up their luggage and getting into cars. There were smiles and a few tears too. The movement rushed by and it seemed to have a kind of rhythm. I waited there quietly, taking it all in, anxious for my new life.

The air was thick and sticky as the sun started to dip down. I wiped sweat from my forehead and thought—at least initially—that the weather wouldn't be a problem for me. I was accustomed to humidity and scorching temperatures. But it was mid-August then. The real test would come when the season changed to winter, and Chicago's nickname, "The Windy City," came into full meaning.

I waited for twenty minutes until a man, a black man, pulled up in an old pick-up truck. He leaned over to roll down the window and looked straight at me.

"Serge?"

I nodded.

He nodded to the bed of the truck.

I tossed my clothes sack into the back and hopped in. I braced the side and waited for him to drive, but he didn't. The man opened his door and got out. He walked alongside the bed and stopped when he reached me. He had a look of confusion on his face.

"What are you doing?" he asked. "In America, you sit up there with me." He pointed to the front of the truck.

"I'm sorry," I said. I hopped down to the curb and got into the front seat.

Back in Africa, the few times I had ever been in a truck were spent in the back. That's how I got to the airport in Khartoum, in fact.

"Make sure you put that seatbelt on, now," he said.

I fastened it as we departed the airport.

"My name's Harold," he said, keeping his eyes on the road.

"Serge," I said.

"I'm a janitor at the school you're going to be attending," he said. "I help them out with whatever odd jobs they have. There's a few extra bucks in it for me."

As we got further away from the airport, I could see the collection of tall buildings drawing near up ahead. It had to be Chicago. There were several buildings like these in Khartoum, but not waves of them like in my new home.

My eyes lit up as we entered into the city, crossing a bridge over a river that never seemed to end. There were several bridges on both sides of the one we were driving across. I rolled my window down and looked up at the buildings. I craned my neck as far back as it could go, looking straight into the blue-purple sky. The buildings seemed to never end, continuing to soar way up above Chicago.

"This your first time here, right?" Harold asked.

"Yes."

"That right there," he said, pointing a thumb

back at the bridge we had just crossed, "is the Chicago River."

When we were stopped at a traffic light, I poked my head out of the window again and took in a lungful of air. I wanted to know what Chicago smelled like. I wanted the air to get inside me. I told myself that I had to be open to new experiences. I couldn't be afraid of them, no matter how scary they seemed.

"You talk pretty good for someone who hasn't been here before," he said.

"In school, when I was young," I said, "I read a lot of books written by American writers. After I stopped going to school, I continued reading."

He nodded and put his eyes back on the road. He didn't say much about the neighborhood that I was going to be living in, just noting that it was on the south side of Chicago. I knew that I would be living with a host family that was arranged by the school. Harold didn't even know that much. All he had was an address.

He stopped the truck and that meant we had arrived in South Side. I came all the way from Sudan and this was the place where I would try to make a new life. There were many people out, all of them black. Some were walking down the sidewalks in pairs or small groups while others stood by, all alone, looking out into the streets. Harold unfastened his seat belt and I sat frozen in the passenger seat staring out of the window and then back at him.

He looked over to me and smiled. "Well, come on now. You can't stay in this truck. Your new home is over there." He pointed to a building across the street.

We got out of the truck.

The first thing that hit me was the noise. There were cars going by with music playing loudly. People walked by, laughing and yelling to each other. And the horns—it seemed like a car horn honked every other second.

Harold handed me my clothes sack and a piece

of paper with the address written on it. He pointed to the building again.

"See you around school," he said, before patting me on the shoulder. "Good luck here in Chi-town."

He got into his truck and waited for a break in the traffic before pulling away from the curb.

I stood there for a moment taking in all of the sound and movement around me.

THREE

"Welcome to Chicago, Serge," she said, after opening the door to the apartment. "My name is Grace."

Grace was my host mother. She had a round face along with a round body. Her smile was warm and inviting. She stepped aside to allow me to enter. I walked in, stopped just past the entrance, and looked around. I never thought that I would be in America, let alone have someone open her home to me. But there I was standing next to Miss Grace, and she seemed happy to have me.

"Let me show you around the apartment," she

said. "It's not a big place, but you'll have your own room."

I followed her around the apartment with my clothes sack over my shoulder as she showed me the kitchen, living room, and dining room. To me, the apartment was a palace. My home in Sudan was a structure made of brick cemented with mud. There were three rooms in my old home: a space that doubled as a kitchen and washroom where my mother and Maya prepared meals and washed clothes—and where the family also ate; a bedroom for my parents and younger siblings; and another for the older children.

Grace led me to my bedroom. She opened the door and I followed her in. She turned a light switch on and my eyes widened when I saw that there was a desk and a dresser inside. I had never had either of these things. The bed stood perfectly in the corner of the room with a small drawer next to it. The drawer had a clock and telephone on top of it. These were new to me as well.

"Put your bag down," she said, nodding to my clothes sack. "Get comfortable. This is your home."

I put it down next to the bed.

"Your clothes go there and you can do homework there," she said, pointing to the dresser and then the desk.

"I've never had my own bed before," I said, slightly embarrassed.

"Well *now* you do."

She left the room and I quickly followed her back into the hallway.

"And here is your bathroom," Grace said as she walked across the hall. "We have our own in our room. This one is just for you. There's cleaning stuff under the sink, a toothbrush, toothpaste and soap right here. And your hand towel is hanging there and your bath towel behind the door."

I smiled after Grace finished talking. She smiled back, though she looked confused.

"What is it, Serge?"

"It's nothing," I said. "I'm just not used to having all of this . . . stuff."

She smiled again and we walked out of the bathroom and back into the hallway.

"Mr. Jones is at work right now," she said. "You'll meet him tonight at dinner."

I felt a swell of gratitude to the school, to Grace and her husband, and to the people who made it possible for me to come to America. I had to prove that I was worthy of this. I had to prove that I deserved all of this kindness.

"You're probably tired," Grace said. "Why don't you lie down for a little bit while I get dinner ready?"

"Okay, Mrs. Jones."

"'Call me 'Grace,'" she said. "Or 'Miss Grace.'"

"Miss Grace?" I called, "Would it be okay if I took a shower?"

She smiled.

"You don't have to ask," she said. "This is your home now."

She left the room, closing the door behind her. I looked around at every corner of the room again. I felt like a king in his castle. I looked down to my clothes sack, unzipped it, and took out a fresh outfit to put on after showering. But before making it to the shower, I laid down in my bed to rest my eyes. Exhaustion took hold, and before I knew it, I was fast asleep.

———

By the time I woke up, it was dark outside. I didn't know what time it was and my head throbbed while I tried to figure it out. Back home, we never used clocks or watches to tell time. We lived according to the sun. When the sun came up, it was time to wake up and go to work. When it went down and the sky turned black, it was time to relax and then sleep. Before I left, a man from my village who had been to America gave me a piece of advice—he said that I should learn to pay attention to clocks. Americans lived by their clocks.

The window was cracked and a breeze cooled the air in my room. I got out of bed and looked out of the window down to the street. Even though it was dark, people were outside—the voices the same, the music still loud. Americans did not let the sun's departure slow them down. If anything, it made them bolder.

Then I tried to listen for Miss Grace and Mr. Jones inside the apartment. I assumed, because it was dark outside, Mr. Jones would be home from work, but I didn't hear him. And the sounds from outside only made the silence inside more noticeable.

There was light coming from the kitchen and dining room, but no voices. I saw the light when I walked to the bathroom. My reflection was tired when I looked into the mirror above the sink. My eyes were still heavy and my thoughts went dreamily back to my family. I wondered what they were doing while I stood there, all alone, in my *own* bathroom in Chicago. I looked down at the sink and saw two handles, one on the right with a 'C' and another on the left with an 'H.' I turned the handle on the right and cold water shot out. I cupped a handful and quickly turned the handle back to the closed position to prevent anymore waste of water. I splashed the water on my face and it shook the sleep right out of me. I left the bathroom.

I walked slowly down the hallway and made my way into the kitchen. Miss Grace and her husband were sitting at a small table with four chairs. The kitchen was small, too, but had a stove and refrigerator—things that we didn't have back in Sudan.

"Serge," Miss Grace said, "I didn't want to bother your sleep. I know you had a long journey."

"Thank you, Miss Grace."

"This is Mr. Jones," she said.

He stood up from the table and I saw that he

was a tall man. He was almost as tall as me and I was six-foot-eight. I wondered if he, too, played basketball when he was younger.

"Serge," he said.

We shook hands and his almost crushed mine.

"Let me make you a plate," Miss Grace said.

Mr. Jones waved for me to sit down and I did so. Miss Grace filled a plate of food for me.

"How does it feel to be in America?" Mr. Jones asked.

"I don't know," I said. "The feeling is still so new."

"It'll get easier," he said, "once you start going to school and playing ball."

His name, "Mike," was stitched onto a patch on his shirt.

"Thanks, Mr. Jones," I said.

"Please," he said. "Call me 'Mike.'"

"Here, you go," Miss Grace said as she set a plate down in front of me.

I looked down and saw a mountain of food.

There was a big pile of meat—what kind, I wasn't sure. And on the side, there were long green beans next to a soft white mound covered with a brown sauce. I leaned my head down to smell the food and it instantly made me feel better. I waited to take my first bite. I was a bit intimidated because I had rarely seen that much food plated for one person before.

"Well, go on and eat," Miss Grace said. "We gotta get some meat on your bones."

She gave me a pat on the shoulder and they both smiled.

I was thin. Miss Grace and Mike both had a little of what she called "meat" on their bones. Back home, though, most people were built like me, and a single person never ate from a plate that had as much food as the one that sat in front of me.

"Thank you," I said.

I took a bite and then another. The meat was tender and well-seasoned. I tried the green beans and they were good, too. I looked up before digging my fork into the white mound.

"What's a matter?" she asked. "You don't like mashed potatoes?"

I shook my head and smiled. I had eaten potatoes many times before in my life, just not covered with a brown sauce.

"I didn't know they were potatoes," I said, before taking a forkful up to my mouth.

"The sauce on top is called 'gravy,'" she said.

"Delicious," I said, after another bite.

By the time I was finished eating, my plate was still half full. I didn't want to be rude during my first day as a guest in their home, but I had no more room.

"Are you done?" she asked.

"Yes," I said. "I don't think I can eat anymore. I'm not used to having this much food for dinner."

Mike continued working on his plate.

"Better yet," she said, as she picked my plate off

of the table along with her own, "save some room for dessert. I made a pecan pie."

I didn't know what pecan pie was exactly, but based on the plate of food that Miss Grace prepared, I knew it would be good too.

"You'll like it," Mike said, before taking another bite of food.

Without being too obvious, I studied him while he ate. He was tall, but also strong. His arms were thick as was his neck.

"Did you ever play basketball, Mike?" I asked. "When you were younger?"

He smiled before putting his fork down.

"I played a little basketball growing up," he said. "But mainly, football was my game. American football."

I knew what American football was, but only vaguely. The only definitive thing I knew about it was that, unlike soccer, you could use your hands.

"Where I come from," I said, "there aren't any basketball players built like you."

"It's a little different here, Serge. You'll see when you get to school."

Miss Grace walked over and put a hand on my shoulder.

"Mike, why don't you take Serge into the living room to watch TV? I'll get dessert ready."

"Okay, baby," he said, before taking his last bite.

Mike's plate was clean as he stood up from the table with a grunt. He walked it over to Miss Grace at the kitchen sink and gave her a kiss on the cheek.

I followed Mike into the living room—another kind of room that I had never experienced back home—and he waved his hand again for me to sit, this time on the soft couch that faced a flat-screen television hanging on the opposite wall.

Mike took a seat on a chair that was next to the couch. The chair looked very soft and comfortable and his body seemed to melt into it. He pulled a lever at its side and his feet kicked out. He let out a sigh of relaxation and he turned on the television. He folded his hands across his bulging stomach and we watched a program about American football in silence. Mike didn't seem eager to exchange words, and neither was I. The program focused on a team called the "Chicago Bears."

When a man on the program began talking about the Bears, Mike sat up in his chair and became animated. He complained about what the Bears lacked and finished his complaint with a remark about how things would never be as they were in 1985. I smiled and nodded whenever Mike looked my way.

Miss Grace walked into the room with a tray in her hands. She set it down on the table in front of the couch and handed a plate to Mike and then one to me. She took a plate for herself and sat down on the couch next to me. Pecan pie turned out to be something tasty as well, just as I'd guessed. It was sweet, though, very sweet, and I could only take a few bites.

After putting my plate down on the tray, I looked around the room and saw several photographs. All of the photos were in frames that were hanging on walls or resting on fixtures. The photos were mostly of Miss Grace and Mike. A few of them were when they were younger and both a bit thinner. A few of them were more recent. There were also a few photos of kids, but they were not together with Miss Grace and Mike in any of them. Miss Grace and Mike seemed to have no children of their own.

"Mike will take you to school tomorrow morning before he goes to work," Miss Grace said, putting her empty plate down on the tray.

"It'll probably take you a few days to learn how to use the buses," Mike said.

"Buses?" I asked.

"Yeah, once you learn the routes, it'll be easy for you to get to school and back," he said.

"One other thing, Serge," she said, putting her

hand on my shoulder again "When it gets dark, you gotta watch yourself out there. Be careful."

She nodded to the open window where the sounds of the street were coming into the room.

FOUR

My new school was an old brick building that took up three blocks of the city. The brick building appeared old and there was a huge cross hanging over the front entrance. I stood in front of it for a while, frozen to the sidewalk. I wore navy blue pants and a white polo shirt underneath a navy blazer. This was my school's required uniform for all students and it had been mailed to Miss Grace before I arrived in Chicago.

I didn't know what to expect that first day. The unknown was exciting for me. I looked at my fellow classmates making their way to the building, and just like me, they were excited to be starting a new school year. Our reasons were different, though. I was happy to be back in school, happy to get back in the classroom after having to quit and work in the fields. I imagined that the other students were happy for different reasons. They laughed and hugged one another and I felt a rise in my chest. I thought about my mother, then about my father and Sefu.

I finally made it into the building. The halls were filled with even more students, and all I could hear was chaos and loud voices. I was supposed to meet my coach— the head coach of the team—before my first class started. To get to my meeting, I tried following a wave of students down the hallway. I towered over the rest of my classmates and could feel their stares as I passed them. No one looked like me in the halls. Many of them had white skin with blonde or brown hair and green or blue eyes. I had noticed right away that mostly black people populated the neighborhood I was living in. This school, though, seemed to be filled mostly with white people. Back home it was very rare to see, let alone speak to, a white person. I walked for several minutes down the crowded hallway before seeing another person with dark skin like me.

When I reached the end of the hallway, the crowd of students thinned. I had a choice to make—go left or right. There weren't any signs on the walls to tell me where to go and only three other students remained in the hall with me. Two of them were together, a boy and a girl, standing close to one another and talking quietly. The other student had blonde hair, too, and was kneeling down to tie his shoe. He stood up and noticed me standing alone. He smiled.

"Hey."

"Hello," I said.

"Do you need some help?"

"I'm just looking for the gym."

"Okay," he said. "School is kinda huge. Is it your first time being here? First day?"

"Yes," I said.

"Follow me."

We walked down the hallway in the direction that I had come from. We passed the main entrance. My mistake was missing the sign that pointed in the gym's direction. The gym was all the way on the other side of the campus. Near the entrance, there was a sign that read "Locker Room," which is where the coach's office was.

"Do you play basketball?" he asked, as I reached for the door to the locker room.

"How could you tell?"

He smiled. "Well, first of all, you were looking for the gym. And second," he looked up at me, "you're really tall."

I smiled. "Yes, I guess those are both good clues."

"What grade are you in?" he asked.

"Eleventh."

"You're on varsity, then?"

I nodded.

"You must be good. Our team is always at the top of the conference, but I guess this year is supposed to be something extra special."

He extended his hand to me.

"My name is Kyle, by the way."

"Serge," I said, shaking his hand.

"Nice to meet you."

"Thanks for your help," I said. "Things are so new. I just got here from Africa yesterday."

"I'd love to hear all about it," he said as a bell rang sharply in the empty hallway. He looked up, waiting for the bell to stop. "I gotta talk to a teacher before that next bell," he said. "I'll look out for you around school." He started walking backwards, away from me. "And Serge, if you ever need any help and I'm not around, just ask. Most people here are really nice."

"Thanks, Kyle."

"See ya around!" he said, before turning and walking back down the hallway.

I watched Kyle walk away until he took a turn out of sight. There was a confidence in the way he walked. I wanted to walk like that one day. I made sure to remember the path from the front door to the locker room. I opened the door and went inside.

———

"How are you liking it in America so far?" Coach asked.

Coach was a short man with thinning brown hair and a full mustache. His arms were short, too, and covered with hair. The only clues that he had a history with the game were his flat stomach and strong forearms. He, too, almost crushed my hand when he shook it. I had to get used to the strong handshakes of Americans.

"It's good, Coach," I said. "It's only been one day. Miss Grace and Mike are very nice."

"Ah, you like them, huh?" he asked. "How's your room?"

"Fine."

"Well, we're happy to have you here," he said. "I haven't seen you play in person, but based on the videos I've seen along with Jerry's recommendation, we think you can really help the team this year. You play with a lot of energy—and you're long as hell. We can't wait to get started with you."

"I do have one question, Coach. What classes will I be taking?" I asked. "I know I will be in the eleventh grade, but other than that—"

"Good question," he said. "I have your class schedule here." He picked up a sheet of paper from his desk and handed it to me.

"One of your teammates named Marvin, who's also an eleventh grader, has the exact same schedule as you. You'll follow him around school this first week."

I nodded and then looked over my schedule.

"And we have a workout after school today, Serge," he said. "We're gonna start in the weight room and then we'll be out on the court."

He checked his watch and his eyes lit up.

"Okay, first period bell is going to ring in two

minutes," he said. "You don't want to be late for your first class."

He stood up from his desk and I did the same. He walked around his desk and led me out to the gym where Marvin was waiting at midcourt. The gym was dark and empty with only faint light coming from windows set high above the floor.

"Marvin is gonna take good care of you, Serge," Coach said, before patting me on the back and giving Marvin the look a father gives a son. Marvin nodded and shook my hand. Coach left us.

I was a few inches taller than Marvin, but his physique told me that he was a low post player like me. I could've been wrong, though. We eyed each other in silence for a few moments.

"They brought you all the way from Africa and gave you a scholarship?"

"Yes." I prepared for a taunt or some kind of other negative response from him, but it didn't come. His face didn't hold any emotion other than the sleepy look in his eyes.

"A'ight, let's get up out of here," he said. "First bell is 'bout to sound off. And you don't wanna be late for first period and shit. Coach'll be all up on your case."

———

We entered our first period classroom. It was English class. I followed Marvin to the back of the classroom and sat down at a desk right next to him. The teacher, a young white woman, called attendance from the front of the room.

I leaned over to Marvin. "Why don't we sit up front?" I asked. "I can't hear the teacher that well from back here."

Marvin looked at me with a relaxed smile. I looked down to the foot of his desk and realized for the first time that he didn't have a book bag. Nothing. No books, no paper, not even a pencil. Before Mike dropped me off at school that morning, Miss Grace surprised me with a backpack, notebooks, pens, and pencils. I carried the back-pack, as well as my gym bag filled with a jersey from my first team in Sudan, gym shorts, and a pair of basketball shoes.

"Cool out. What's your name again?" he asked. "Sarge? Surge?"

"Serge."

"We sit back here so we can chill," he said.

When the teacher called my name, the classroom became silent. I responded in a low voice with "Present," and the rest of the people in class turned their heads in unison to the back of the classroom. There were glances of surprise when it was realized that the soft voice in the back came from someone who was six-foot-eight. But as quickly as the moment came, it also passed. Everyone turned back around and looked to the teacher again. I survived it.

The teacher welcomed us to the official start of the school year and talked about what we were going to cover during the two semesters. When

I figured out that we were not going to do any work that day, my mind drifted back to home. I thought of my first English class when I was eight years old. When growing up in Sudan, one had to be able speak the two national languages of Arabic and English, as well as the indigenous language of their tribe. I got a late start on English because there wasn't a teacher who knew it well enough at the school I attended. That changed when I turned eight and we got a new teacher. She was a young white woman from America, named Miss Sobel, who came to my village to teach English to the children. The first English book she ever gave us was *The Jungle Book* by Rudyard Kipling. The copy that I received was brand new with a hard cover and pristine, crisp, pages. I had never seen something so new and promised myself to keep it in that condition. The story never got old for me, even as we moved on to to other books in class. I read *The Jungle Book* four times that year, sometimes by candlelight, learning something new each time. I held onto that book as tight as I could. Miss Sobel was the first person to ever give me a book—the first person to ever give me anything, really—and I would never forget that.

I was nine-and-a-half years old, just about to quit school, when Miss Sobel left our village. I remembered being very sad about it. On her last day of class, she asked to see my copy of *The Jungle Book*, which was worn from constant use. When I gave it to her, she took out a pen and wrote something inside the front cover. She handed the book back to me and told me to wait until I got home to read what she wrote. When I did get home later that day and flipped open the cover, I could not believe what she had written to me. No one had ever said anything like that to me. The words, her words, became a constant voice in my head. I heard those words when my father told me that I had to quit school and again when I had to decide if I was going to come to America to play basketball. She wrote:

Dear Serge,

This book was given to you with love and peace in mind. But it's you and your classmates who have given me a gift. Thank you. It's been a joy having you as a student.

Sincerely,
Miss Sobel

P.S. Your imagination will set you free.

By the time I turned fifteen, I had read *The Jungle Book* probably fifty times. And every time I read it, I made sure to flip open the front cover and look at Miss Sobel's note.

When the bell rang and English class was over, Marvin was fast asleep in the back. The teacher didn't seem to mind. She didn't say anything about him to the class or even try to wake him up. I tapped him on the shoulder. He shifted, opened his eyes, and wiped the drool from the side of his mouth.

"Come on," he said, stretching his arms out. "Let's move it on out."

He slept through the next two classes before lunch, including—incredibly—physical education. In the cafeteria, he was wide-awake, bouncing from table to table, slapping high fives with boys and hugging the girls. I didn't follow him around during lunch and he didn't ask me to. I sat alone eating a hamburger and fries, which the school provided to me for free. I looked around the cafeteria for Kyle in between bites, but didn't see him.

After lunch, I was excited to see that my pre-Algebra teacher, Mr. Sesay, was black like me. And what made it even better was that he, too, was of African descent. I liked math as a young boy and was pretty good at it too, but because I left school so young, most of the concepts had slipped my memory.

"You'll catch up in no time," Mr. Sesay said, as we chatted after class.

He was an inspiration to me because, just like

me, he had come to Chicago alone when he was sixteen years old. He said that if I ever needed to talk to just knock on his door. It would always be open to me. I shook his hand and walked out of the classroom. Marvin was outside talking to a girl and waiting for me. He nodded lazily when I approached.

"Just one more to go," he said with a sigh.

I realized that one day of following Marvin around school would be enough. I would handle myself from then on.

The last class of the day was art class. The teacher was another young woman who looked to be of high-school age herself. She explained to us that her class would cover a spectrum of traditions, disciplines, and theories. "We aren't going to just paint and draw," she said, her eyes gleaming in the low light of art studio 'A,' "we are going to paint, draw, write poetry, write short stories, daydream and even make short films." This sounded exciting to me.

Marvin was well on his way to daydreaming in the back of that class, just like all the classes before. When the final bell rang, he opened his eyes and stretched out his limbs again. He smiled with squinted eyes.

"Finally," he said.

I followed him to the locker room. The sound of rap music mixed with the back-and-forth hollering of my new teammates filled the air inside.

FIVE

I kept to myself while I changed into my practice uniform. Most of the other guys talked and joked, while a few others were quiet like me. Marvin was the only other player that I'd been introduced to. Their silence towards me didn't make me feel uncomfortable. Being the new guy from a strange place, I kind of expected it. But I also didn't know how to reach out. I would wait to meet the rest of my teammates out on the floor, where I was most comfortable.

A tall and very thin white man with a full head of blonde hair passed through the locker room without stopping or speaking to anyone. He looked like the man who recruited me to Chicago from Sudan—Jerry Torshiano.

I didn't believe that Jerry would walk into the locker room and not say anything to me, but I had to make sure. I followed the man out of the locker room and to the back of the school. The man was standing behind the open trunk of a car in the parking lot. He closed the trunk and hung a gym bag around his shoulder. I walked over to the car to see if this man was Jerry. When I got close enough to him, I realized that it was not. He just looked like Jerry, though.

"Everything, okay?" the man asked as he started walking back toward the locker room door.

"Oh . . . yes," I said. "You look like someone I know. Someone from back in Africa."

"Africa, huh?" he asked. "I've never been there before."

"Sorry."

"It's no problem. Say, what's your name?"

"Serge."

"Nice to meet you, Serge," the man said and shook my hand. "My name is Mr. Prindell. I teach Chemistry and also coach volleyball."

That explained the gym bag around his shoulder.

"You're here all the way from Africa?"

"Yes."

"And this man," he said, "the one that looks like me. He helped you come here?"

"He is the main reason I'm here," I said.

He thought about that and nodded.

"Well, I'm sure you have a workout soon," he said. "You look like a basketball player; am I right?"

"Yes, sir," I said.

We walked back into the locker room and Mr. Prindell stopped at a fork in the path. To the left were my teammates and the loud music. To the right it was empty and quiet.

"Where does your team practice?" I asked.

"Oh, we use a small gym on the other side of campus," he said. "The volleyball team, and all of the girls athletic teams really—they don't create much of a buzz around here."

"I don't understand," I said. "Buzz?"

"Just wait until the first home basketball game of the season," he said, pointing to the doorway that led to the gym. "You'll see what I mean."

"I have to go, Mr. Prindell," I said, pointing a thumb back to where the rest of my teammates were.

"Good luck, Serge," he said.

"Thank you."

He walked to the right and disappeared into the dark rows of lockers.

I walked back over to where my teammates were and saw Marvin sitting in front of his locker. There were still some guys getting ready and those who were ready continued talking.

"Are we going to start soon?" I asked.

"We still got some time. Just waitin' on Rodney," Marvin said. "He's in a meeting with Coach.

Rodney's our best player, in case you didn't know. We don't do shit around here without Rodney."

I turned away from Marvin and went to an empty row of lockers away from the rest of the guys. I sat in front of the first one on the end of the row. Feeling the fatigue from my trip catching up to me, I closed my eyes, but I didn't fight it. I let my mind drift away.

When I was fifteen years old, Jerry Torshiano discovered me at a basketball camp in Khartoum. Luol Deng, a player on the Chicago Bulls and native son of Sudan, sponsored the camp. I met Luol through the first coach I ever played for in Darfur. After seeing me play once, he invited me to his camp. When I first arrived, I was nervous to the point of not even being able to step on the court. The players from my village weren't all that skilled. The players who had gathered in the city of Khartoum looked like they had all been playing for years. I knew it wasn't going to be as easy for me to stand out. I wasn't sure how

I would do against these other players from all across Africa—players who were more experienced, confident, and athletically gifted than me.

The camp began, and to my surprise, I was able to hold my own. Fatigue never bothered me during the sessions. I could play games all day in the heat and still be fresh enough to practice extra at night. I gained confidence in my game with each second that passed. By the end of camp I was named MVP of the tournament, and as a result, received Nike shoes and workout clothes. The shoes were nice, but the event that really changed things happened on the final day of camp. Luol had heard about my improvement and invited me to play in the counselors' game that marked the end of camp. The counselors were made up of college players from America, along with a small group of Luol's fellow players from the NBA. I was honored to play in that game on the last night of camp in front of all the campers as well as talent scouts from across America and Europe.

I blocked six shots during the counselors' game—even getting one of Luol's—and scored ten points along with twelve rebounds. After the game, Luol introduced me to many of the scouts. Jerry was the one who took the most interest in me. He said he loved my length and energy. He knew that my offensive game was raw. Because I could rebound and block shots so well, though, there was an opportunity to be an instant contributor on a high school team in America. He specifically mentioned one in Chicago that had a need for a tall, athletic forward. I had a good feeling about Jerry from that first meeting. He looked me directly in the eyes and treated me with respect. That was the first time I ever thought that a life outside of Sudan might exist for me.

A day after the camp ended, Luol said that all of the scouts from America—and a few from Europe and Canada—were interested in me. I told Luol that the only one I wanted to hear from was Jerry Torshiano.

Luol set up a meeting that day, before I was to go back to Darfur. During the meeting, Jerry explained to me that he worked with several high schools back in the States. He could've gotten me into schools in New York City, Connecticut, or Chicago. But, like the first time I talked to him, the school in Chicago seemed to be the best fit.

When I asked Luol what he thought, he smiled.

"Is there even a question where you should go?" he asked.

That was enough for me. We all agreed that Chicago was the choice, if for no other reason than Luol's relationship with the city. If I ever needed him he would be there to help, and, more importantly, Luol was someone who had succeeded in what I was attempting to do—make it out of Sudan.

Jerry told me that he would secure everything with the school in Chicago and then get in touch with Luol. Luol would then get word to me in Darfur. If I accepted the scholarship and decided that I could go through with moving away, Chicago would be my new home.

Before Jerry left the meeting in Khartoum, he looked me in the eyes and told me that I would make it in America. He also thought that I had a chance to secure a college scholarship if I put in the work. Those words meant a lot, and with Luol's support and guidance, I felt like leaving Sudan was something that I could actually do. America wasn't just this place in my mind anymore, a place that I had read about in books, it was real. I could almost touch it. Getting a college education in America? More than I ever dreamed of.

Luol got back to me about a month later. I was out in the fields with my father and Sefu when the message came. My mother cried when she found out that I had the opportunity to go to America to play basketball. My father didn't say anything. Neither did Sefu.

About six months before I was to depart for America, Luol was traded from the Chicago Bulls to Cleveland Cavaliers. He would not be in Chicago to look over me after all. I *was* going to stay with him at his home before he was traded, but that was no longer an option. Luol worked with the school in Chicago to ensure that I would have a safe place to live. That's where Miss Grace and Mike came in.

These thoughts disappeared from my mind as Marvin walked over. He let me know that Rodney was there and that it was time to lift weights. I felt thankful for Luol, thankful for Jerry Torshiano, and thankful for Miss Grace and Mike. I was thankful for having them all in my life. I had a lot of expectations to live up to.

Our first pre-season workout started in the weight room. They split us up into two groups: guards and "bigs." There were twelve of us, which was the standard number for a basketball team. It appeared that no one was in danger of being cut. This was our team.

I had never lifted weights before. I didn't work on my strength in Africa because we relied more on our speed and athleticism. This was different. Standing there looking at the guys on the team made me remember what Mike said the night before. My teammates—every one of them—were bulky with well-defined, bulging muscles. I was the only skinny one.

The strength and conditioning coach, a man named Gene, was a stout, thick man with no neck. It looked like his head was connected to his shoulders. He prowled from station to station in the weight room, encouraging some players and ridiculing others for their inability to get the weight up. For that session we were instructed to just work on our legs because arm exercises would throw the shooting off once we hit the floor. We would do arm lifts on days that we didn't have on-court work.

While waiting in line to do squats, a couple of the other "bigs" introduced themselves. Well, *kind of* introduced themselves. They all mentioned that they had heard about me but weren't sure if I was really coming over. One of them, Cornelius, was the starting center from the year before. He was six-foot-ten without an ounce of fat on his body.

"Where you from?" Cornelius asked.

"Africa. Sudan, actually."

"Fo' real? You mean *Africa*, Africa?"

I nodded.

"Yes. *Africa*, Africa."

Gene approached our group when it was my turn to do squats. All of the guys in front of me did squats with the same amount of weight. I didn't want to look weak in their eyes, so I kept that same amount on the bar.

I took my stance and rested the bar on my shoulders.

"Come on, Sudan!" Gene yelled. "Show me what you got!"

The rest of the guys laughed.

I inhaled and took all of the weight on my shoulders. My legs bent slowly. Once I got down into a squat position, they began to shake. There was no way that I was going to be able to come up and complete the lift. The weight was too much for my skinny frame.

"Come on, Sudan!" Gene barked. "Come on!"

I had a decision to make. I could either try to lift the weight and risk falling backward or give up and let the bar roll off my back. It was an easy decision.

"What are you doing?" Gene asked.

The bar banged coldly into a rack, sending a clang through the entire weight room. The rest of the guys turned their heads my direction. When they saw that I had fallen to the floor, they came over to see if I was okay. I picked myself up slowly, carefully, to make sure I was in one piece. The rest of the team along with Gene formed a semi-circle around me.

"Make sure you have the right weight on there," Marvin said with a smirk. "You need to get a little muscle on them li'l African bones before you lift with the big boys." Everyone in the semi-circle laughed and then spread back out around the weight room.

Gene pulled me aside.

"It's okay," he said. "You're not used to lifting like this."

"No, I'm not."

"You gotta catch up physically to the rest of the guys at your position if you wanna see the floor," he said. "We are a pretty strong team as you can see."

"They don't have guys like this playing basketball where I come from."

"You just gotta work a little harder," he said, "to make up for lost time."

I nodded.

Gene smiled and gave me a thick chop on the shoulder.

"You work with me for the rest of this session," he said. "I'll show you all the lifts and you can do them with light weight."

"Okay, Mr—"

"Just 'Gene.'"

"Gene."

I followed Gene around the weight room for the last thirty minutes of the session. He showed me how to do all of the leg lifts. He showed me how to balance the bar properly so I wouldn't hurt my back. He showed me how to grip the bar on squats and dead lifts. And finally, he showed me the chart hanging on the wall where I was to record my progress.

After the lift, we had a fifteen-minute break to drink Gatorade and eat energy bars—luxuries back home, but plentiful here. Most of the guys went to the training room to tape their ankles. I didn't need my ankles taped. I went out on the court early to practice free throws.

I was on one end shooting free throws and the rest of the team was on the other waiting for practice to begin. Coach came out and gathered us up at midcourt. He welcomed us to the new season and introduced me to the rest of the team.

"I want everyone on the team to make Serge feel welcome," he said. "Make him feel like family."

As Coach spoke, some of the guys rolled their eyes and others grinned as they looked me up and down.

It was embarrassing to be singled out just because I was new and from a different place. I didn't want any extra attention because of where I was from. I wanted to earn my place on the team. I wanted to earn the respect of my teammates. I knew that by calling me out, Coach was just going to make my job harder. I wondered for a moment if he had done it on purpose.

We started with warm-ups and stretching.

Rodney quietly led the team in stretching. There was something in his eyes that I didn't see in the rest of the guys. I also realized that he wasn't one of the guys that was laughing and joking around in the weight room. He seemed liked he stayed to himself, just like me.

After the stretches, we started with a variety of shooting drills. When it was my turn, I could feel everyone's eyes on me. A few times there were comments followed by laughs. It didn't help matters that my shooting was off that day. Shooting was the weakest part of my game. Combined with my struggles in the weight room, I knew there would always be something to work on in my free time.

Coach offered encouragement with each shot I missed. That just added to the tension. The guys were eying me after every move, sizing me up, trying to figure out if I could actually play or if I was just some experiment in Coach's head.

We moved to defense and rebound drills. I was excited for this because these were the two parts of my game that were most developed. The constant discomfort that came with staying low in a defensive stance was nothing to me. Working on the farm with my dad and Sefu was more demanding than being in a defensive stance could ever be. On the sugarcane fields there was no other choice but to continue working, no matter how much pain or discomfort you were in, no matter how sore your back and hands were. Pain was nothing to me.

My feet and calves on fire was nothing to me.

This was easy.

After basic stance work—sliding from side to side and up and back—we worked on man-to-man defense. My first matchup was against another post player named Charlie. He could handle the ball pretty well for a big guy. I decided to crowd him so he wouldn't feel comfortable dribbling the ball in front of me. I also wanted to set the tone in front of the rest of the team. I wanted them to see that when I was defending, it would be a challenge to get past me. Charlie wasn't ready for my quick feet.

Anywhere he went, I was there in front of him. I was able to anticipate his movements and—because he had no other choice—he settled for a deep jump shot that I got a finger on. The shot fell weakly out of the air, nowhere near the rim.

My next two one-on-one's came against Cornelius. Because he played center, the actions started with a pass down to him in the post. Even though he had size and strength on me, I didn't back down mentally, and more importantly, didn't give up any ground physically. He tried to bump me and knock me off balance, but my footwork was too good. He dropped his back foot and I knew what was coming next—the drop step. I gave a little ground, and when he went up for the shot, I elevated and blocked it with the tip of my left hand. Feeling angry, Cornelius came at me a little harder the second time. He tried the drop step again—the same, exact move—except this time he led with his elbow and it connected with my forehead. I fell to the floor and there was stinging right behind my eyes. Coach blew his whistle, calling an offensive foul on Cornelius. Cornelius threw the ball down to the other end of the gym as I patted my nose and forehead to check for blood. There wasn't any. Coach sent Cornelius off to cool down. Before doing so, he told him to help me up off the floor. I didn't need anyone's help getting up, though. I popped up, and in an effort to cool down, took a few steps away. Cornelius walked off the floor to the sideline and one of the assistant coaches followed him and talked in his ear. He turned around—the assistant coach still at his side—and began pacing up and down the sideline, staring at me.

I didn't let this slow me down. The rebounding drills went even better for me. When it was my turn to box out during the drills, no one got a rebound over me. When I was being boxed out, I used my speed to get the rebound every time. I loved rebounding.

There's something special about rebounding. I

spoke these words in my head, while waiting in line for my next turn. I made sure to speak these thoughts in English. *It doesn't take skill. You just have to go get the ball. And when you are boxing out, you have to do anything you can to not let your man get the ball.*

I had memorized that from a book on basketball that I borrowed from a library in Sudan.

I could see, that at the very least, guys were taking note of what I did well. I didn't get any words or pats on the back from them, but I could feel something change.

At the end of practice there was a scrimmage. Coach divided us up. To my shock, I took the floor with the starters. Coach instructed me to stay out of the way on offense because I didn't know any of the plays.

"Just go after offensive rebounds," he said. "But on defense, though, I want you to take over!"

Any time the ball came to me during the scrimmage, I quickly tried to find a safe pass to a teammate. I realized just how good Rodney was on that end of the floor. He was a smooth player that didn't rush. He handled the ball with ease and made running the team look even easier. If a defender crowded him, he used his speed to go by him. If the defender gave him space, he would just pull up for an easy jump shot. And if two defenders came at him, he just found the open man.

On one memorable offensive possession, Rodney went past his man and my guy went over to help. He gave me a perfect bounce pass and I finished the play with a two-handed dunk. As we ran down to the other end, he pointed at me. I pointed back.

"What's your name?" he asked as we got back on defense.

"Call me Sudan," I joked.

"Nah, what's your real name?"

"Serge."

"Cool. I'm Rodney."

I got all of the rebounds on defense and blocked

five shots. The other side was having trouble with my length. When a player drove past his guy thinking there was a clear lane to the basket, I flashed from the weak-side and wiped the shot away. The frustration grew on the other side as I took over the scrimmage. It felt good. It felt like I was already doing my job—that I was earning my place.

On the last possession, Rodney got free again and went up for the shot. I could see that the ball was going to roll off the rim. I got around the box out easily, and slammed the ball with one hand.

The buzzer sounded and our side won the scrimmage by fifteen points. Rodney gave me a high five, and following his lead, the rest of my side did so as well.

Coach called the team up to midcourt again.

"I appreciate the intensity," he said. "Rodney. Serge. You two were phenomenal."

The rest of the guys clapped, but it was probably more so for Rodney than for me.

"Rodney," he said. "Break us down."

The circle got tighter and Rodney lifted one arm into the air. We all did the same.

"Defense on three! Defense on three!" Rodney said. "One! Two! Three!"

"Defense!"

Coach pulled me aside after the rest of the team had scattered back to the locker room.

"Remember Harold?" he asked. "He'll give you a ride home. But you have to hurry so he can get home in time to see his kids."

"That's okay, Coach," I said. "I want to go back into the weight room."

"Now?"

"Yes."

"That was one hell of a workout we just had."

"I need to get stronger."

"How will you get home?"

"I'll find my way."

"Okay," he said with a smile.

I walked into the locker room and changed into my workout clothes that I had in my gym bag.

My jersey from Sudan was white with the black, red, and green of the flag. Marvin laughed when I turned around and Cornelius just stood there with anger still in his eyes.

I put my eyes down.

"You goin' out dressed like that?" Marvin asked through that awful grin of his.

"No."

"You goin' back out to the gym?" he asked.

"I'm going to lift," I said quietly.

I walked past them.

"Sudan!" Marvin said.

I turned around and looked back at him.

"I see you kissing Coach's ass. Be careful, though. You don't wanna cross niggas from Chicago. This ain't Sudan."

Cornelius continued to stare me down.

"What do you mean?" I asked.

Marvin nodded to the empty locker room.

"These niggas in here," he said, "they'll play along right now, cause this is preseason and none of this shit matters. But if you pull this shit during the season, you're gonna have problems."

I didn't say anything to that.

"And I'm not talkin' about the kind of problems you're used to," he said. "Runnin' from cheetahs and lions and shit."

Cornelius laughed and Marvin did too.

I tried to look them in the eyes as they laughed at me, but couldn't. I had to get stronger first. I turned my back and left the locker room. I walked into the dark, empty weight room and turned on the light. I thought about Marvin's warning. Following him around school that day taught me a lot about him. Watching him sleep through every class told me that he wasn't someone that I should be following. It didn't make sense that he would take the opportunity of being at a good school so lightly. Rodney, on the other hand, seemed like someone worth getting to know, but I had to gain more of his respect on the court. That first practice was a start, but there was more work to do.

I put weight on both sides of the bar. I got into the proper position that Gene had shown me earlier and started doing squats. I didn't worry about anything while I lifted weights, alone. Where I came from, my family, my past—none of it mattered in there or on the floor. I was just a player, no different than any other one.

SIX

After finishing in the weight room, I looked around for someone to ask directions from outside of school. The sun was down now and there weren't many people out on the streets. The smell of food was in the air, pouring from a restaurant across the street. I couldn't exactly say what kind of food it was, but the restaurant's sign read, "Greek—American Food." There was a man smoking a cigarette off to the side of the entrance. I crossed the street and approached him. He was an older white man with white hair and relaxed eyes. He had an apron on that was spattered with all different colors. He smoked his cigarette and eyed me.

"Excuse me," I said. "I don't know where I am going."

"Well get in line, kid."

"I have this," I said, handing him the slip of paper with Miss Grace's address.

He took it and examined it.

"It's a South Side address. This is South Side," he said, pointing down toward the sidewalk.

A siren went off in the distance that seemed to be both coming near and moving away at the same time.

"You could walk," he said, "or take the bus. You only need one bus to this address. You need money for the bus."

I looked down to the sidewalk. "I don't have any."

"Well, looks like you're gonna be walkin', kid."

"Which direction?"

"You see, this is 77th Street," he said, pointing

to the sign above the street about fifteen feet away. "Walk down to 76th, which is one block thataway, and take a left. Then walk, oh, eight, ten blocks down and when you get to Halstead, stop. This address is at 76th Street and Halstead."

He handed the slip of paper back to me.

"Thank you."

"No sweat, kid."

I walked toward the street sign and heard a whistle from behind me. I turned around.

"One more thing," he said. "Watch yourself once you get around Halstead. The sun's gone down."

I turned back around and started home.

———

I didn't understand why the man had warned me. Miss Grace had given me the same warning the night before. There were people out on the streets—men, women, even some boys—and they were laughing and talking with each other. There was loud rap music playing from apartment windows and passing cars. There were some people with bottles in their hands, but they weren't causing any trouble.

Why was I being warned?

Warnings were common in Sudan, and you paid close attention to them because if you didn't, you were dead. Life was cheap there. Not like it was in America. From my perspective, I saw very little to fear on the streets of Chicago.

I recognized Miss Grace's building on Halstead and used the stairs to reach the third floor where the apartment was. There was the thick smell of meat in the hallway and it grew stronger as I got closer to the door. I knocked on the door and heard the heavy steps behind it.

———

"Why didn't you take the bus?" Miss Grace asked as she plated rice and beans out of a big pot on the stove.

I sat alone at the table. Mike had just gotten home from work and was showering.

"It didn't take long," I said.

Mike walked into the kitchen and took two bowls from Miss Grace. He came to the table and set one for me and one for himself.

"You should learn the buses," he said, before going back for a third bowl. "It's fine now because the weather is nice, but come November, you don't want to be outside any more than you have to."

He set the third bowl on the table for Miss Grace and sat down.

"I'll learn them," I said. "Thank you."

Miss Grace joined us and began to eat. We all did. And the food was good. It was so good that no one said a word for the next five minutes.

"What's wrong with Halstead?" I asked, breaking the silence.

Miss Grace and Mike looked at each other and smiled.

"Since I've been here, people have been telling me to be careful. Miss Grace told me last night. And another man today."

"It's a hard question to answer," he said.

Miss Grace cleared her throat.

"What Mike is trying to say, Serge, is that our boys here in South Side can be tough," she said. "Some of them are just angry. About what? It's hard to say. But they're angry."

She paused.

"And they don't know what to do with all that anger. So you, we, all the *good* people in the neighborhood," she said. "Suffer a little bit from it. All that anger."

I nodded and looked down at my plate. Suddenly I wasn't hungry anymore.

We finished in silence and I took the trash out

before going to my room. When I laid down in bed, my eyes closed tight the first chance they got. I heard cars going by on Halstead along with some yelling in the street before I drifted away.

———

I could hear the anger in their voices as they called into my father's hut. I could hear the sounds of English swear words and vicious laughs cut by the idling engines of their off-road Jeeps. I knew that they were pressuring my father—not because he told me they were, but because Sefu had said. My father would never give in to their pressures, no matter how ugly the threats became or how close they came to coming true. The late night harassment was happening more and more. When they showed up in their Jeeps, my mother and the rest of my siblings would sneak out in the dark under dim moonlight and hide in a shed out back that my father, Sefu, and I built with our bare hands. It got to the point that the shed became the place where my mother and siblings slept. It wasn't safe or prudent to have them sleep in the house anymore. The only people who stayed out front in the hut were me, my father, and Sefu. I wasn't scared because my father and brother weren't scared. I thought that these people were coming in the night to try to steal from my dad in some way, to take one of his few animals or the little money he had in his pocket. He'd never back down from them. I knew that deep in my heart.

The night that it happened was much like the others, except that my mother and siblings weren't in the shed. They were at my uncle's hut in a different part of the village. I could hear the Jeeps idling out front. And then I heard the yelling, the insults, the threats. Threats that they were going to come inside and burn everything down. My father took hold of his machete. My brother Sefu, with his own machete, stood right next to him. I asked where mine was and they told me to leave the hut, to go out back, to run into the woods and not stop until I got somewhere safe.

I told them that I wanted to stay and they insisted that I couldn't. They didn't give me an explanation, and I didn't ask for one. Time was running short. "Go out to the woods, Serge. Now!" I stepped to the back door and turned to look back. I saw my father approach the front door. My brother was right behind him. They looked back at me and nodded. It was pitch black outside. There was no sound. It seemed like time stood still for a few moments. Jeeps quickly swallowed the silence. I went into the brush behind the hut, but not too deep. I heard my father shout, then heard shouts of anger from the men. Finally, I heard the shots.

———

I gasped for air as sirens screamed outside my Chicago window. I didn't know where I was at first. I sat up in bed and saw four empty, white walls. The air in the room was cool and I looked over to see that the window was cracked. I got up out of bed and walked over to the window. The view outside jogged my memory. The sounds of the sirens came from a block down on Halstead. There were three police cars surrounding another car. The glowing red and blue lights jumped and spun, threatening the night.

SEVEN

I borrowed a few dollars from Miss Grace to catch the bus to school the next morning. I told her that I would pay her back. She just smiled and said that it was no problem.

Mike pointed me to a bus stop on Halstead near the apartment. I could stay on that one bus until it stopped right in front of school. I waited for five minutes until the bus arrived. It was crowded, but I found a small spot in the back to stand.

I craned my neck to look out of the window as the bus stopped and started, as it picked people up and let them off. I could see the massive buildings of downtown Chicago in the distance. They seemed miles and miles away, even though they weren't. The nightmares about my father and Sefu were the same. They were in a distant world that only came to life when I closed my eyes.

Basketball was my peace. When I wasn't on the floor, though, there was a terrible feeling inside of me—a feeling that had to do with the past. It haunted me. I couldn't figure out why the nightmares struck when they did. The last one came after a good day. I didn't want to move on from my life in Sudan. What I wanted was to let go of the pain. I wanted the nightmares to stop. The only problem was I didn't know how to make them stop.

The bus stopped right in front of school and the sight of it shook me out of my thoughts. I hurried to exit through the back door.

Kyle was in front of school talking to a girl that I recognized from one of my classes. She smiled and said "hello" to me before going inside. Kyle shook my hand.

"Serge."

"What's up, Kyle?"

"Just waiting out front," he said. "Hoping to run into you."

"Is something wrong?"

"No, not at all," he said. "I just wanted to make sure that everything is going smoothly for you here at school. I give tours to kids that are thinking of coming to school here and when we have students from other countries, I try to help them out as well."

"Thanks," I said. "But I think I'm starting to get comfortable."

"Glad to hear it," he said. "Anytime you need something, just ask."

His insistence caused me to think for a moment.

"There is one thing," I said. "I need a job."

"A job." he said, his chin in his hand. He snapped his finger.

"Got it! They need help after school in the Admissions Office with answering the phones, copying brochures, stuff like that. I'll talk to the principal."

"Thanks, Kyle."

"No problem."

We walked into school right before first bell.

———

School went by and I enjoyed all of my classes, especially because there was no need to follow Marvin around again. He slept in the back of every class by himself. I sat in the front of class during every period. I ran into Kyle again during lunch and he told me to go to the Admissions Office after school to talk to a Mrs. Fowler. When the last bell rang, I went to the office and spoke to her. After showing me around the office and noting what my responsibilities would be, she gave me the job. I would start the next day, right after school.

I went by Coach's office after I saw Mrs. Fowler.

He was sitting at his desk writing something down.

I knocked on the open door before entering. He looked up and waved me in.

"Serge," he said. "Come on in."

I sat down in front of him.

"What's up?"

"I just wanted to tell you that I got a job."

"A job?" he asked. "Where?"

"Here at school. In the Admissions Office."

"You know that during the season there won't be time for you to work?"

"I know," I said. "I want to work after school for a couple of hours on the days that we don't have practice."

"You mean when we just have weight-lifting?" he asked.

I nodded.

"But when the season starts, you'll have to quit the job, Serge."

"I understand," I said. "I just need a little bit

of money right now. And I don't want to ask my host family. They've done enough already."

Coach smiled. "That's very responsible of you," he said.

He put his eyes down to the sheet he was writing on.

"That's fine, Serge. On the days that we don't have practice out on the floor, you can lift after you finish your work in the Admissions Office."

I smiled.

He put a finger in the air. "But you have to make sure that you lift every day. No excuses."

"I will, Coach."

"Okay."

I got up and left his office. I was happy that he had given me his blessing. I needed to make a little bit of money for myself, and it was another way to keep me busy and keep my mind off the nightmares.

There was also one other bonus: I would be

able to lift weights now without my teammates watching me struggle.

———

We just had weight lifting that day, but my plan was to ask Rodney if he wanted to take some extra jump shots with me after we were done. Gene was waiting for me in the weight room when I entered. He wanted to show me all of the upper body lifts before I tried them out on my own.

"Ready to work on those skinny arms of yours?" he asked with a smile.

"Yes."

We started with the bench press. Gene put two forty-five pound weights on each side of the bar. He slid underneath and lifted the bar off of the rack. His chest expanded and he exhaled as he pushed the bar up and brought it back down. He did this fifteen times with ease.

"Okay," he said, not breathing hard at all. "Your turn."

I took one forty-five pound weight off of each side. I slid underneath the rack and took a deep breath.

"Now make sure you inhale when you bring the bar down and exhale when you push it up," he said, taking his position behind the rack to spot me. "It's the proper way to do it."

I lifted the bar off of the rack and the weight shifted unevenly as I pushed the bar up.

"Okay. Okay," he said. "Now ease it back down."

I brought the bar down and it took all the strength I had to stop the bar from crushing my chest.

I tried to push the weight back up for a second time, but my arms were already dead. Gene quickly lifted the bar up with ease back into the rack.

I sat up, out of breath.

"You see how the bar was moving all over the place?" he asked.

I nodded.

"You have to make sure you keep your hands at an equal distance apart," he said. "That keeps the weight balanced."

"I don't think I'll ever be able to lift as much as you."

He smiled. "That takes a lot of work. You're just getting started here. As long as you stay with it, you'll get stronger."

I didn't say anything. I just let his words sink in.

"Even though you only did one bench press rep today, it's growth," he said. "And tomorrow you do two, and the next day, three. Every moment we're in here, we're learning something."

When there was a little break, I walked over to where the guards were and watched them finish their lifts. Rodney was on the bench press and the rest of his group was circled around. He had two-hundred-thirty-five pounds on the bar and lifted it sixteen times by my count. He made it look easy. After he racked the bar, he called out to one of the other guards, saying, "Beat that!"

When the circle broke apart, I walked over to him at the bench press.

"What's up?" I said.

"Hey Serge," he said, before standing up from the bench.

"Do you want to go shoot some jumpers? I am working on my jump shot, and—"

"We're not supposed to shoot after we do upper body lifts," he said. "But fuck it. Gimme ten and I'll meet you out there."

"Okay," I said.

He left the weight room.

I turned around and Marvin was there, staring at me along with a couple of the other guys. I nodded but they didn't say anything. They just kept staring. I put my head down and walked past them out of the weight room.

I got out onto the floor first and Rodney met me right after. He was right; my first ten shots missed badly because of the arm lifts. It took ten minutes for my arms to feel normal again.

Rodney didn't shoot at first. He just rebounded for me. When it was time for him to shoot, he walked over to me with the ball in his hands.

"I know a few of the guys are giving you trouble," he said. Rodney wasn't around in the locker room the day before, when Marvin and Cornelius were starting problems with me.

"How do you know?" I asked.

He smiled. "I know everything that goes on with the team."

He stepped out to about fifteen feet and took his first shot. It swished through the net perfectly.

"I'm the leader," he said.

Out of twenty shots, Rodney hit eighteen. His shooting form was fluid; he used his legs when he shot and as he brought the ball higher to its release point there was no wasted motion. After each shot, he let his right hand hang in the air as a signal of success.

When it was my turn to shoot again, I noticed that my form was not fluid at all. My legs weren't working together with my arms. I never learned how to shoot properly in Sudan. I *did* learn from Rodney on that day, though, just from watching him. I learned that every part of the body needs to be in sync in order to have a good jump shot.

Rodney shot twenty more and made sixteen of them. He made it look easy, not even breaking a sweat. I couldn't wait to see what he could do in a game against another team.

On my last set of shots, I focused on my form rather than the result of the shot. It felt awkward at first because I was used to doing it the wrong way.

I made thirteen out of twenty shots on my last turn, including the last eight. Rodney didn't say anything to me about my new shooting form, but I'm sure he noticed. He noticed everything.

After my last shot, we walked off the floor.

"I got your back, Serge," he said. "And you're gonna help us win a championship this year."

EIGHT

I took the bus home and no one was there when I walked in. I used the key that Miss Grace had given me. It felt good to have her and Mike's trust. It was hard to trust people other than your family in Sudan. There were a lot of people offering things in return for your trust and there were also people who took your trust by force.

Miss Grace left a note on the dining room table that said that she and Mike would be out for the night and that there was some food in the refrigerator for me. I ate and washed the dishes that I used as well as the ones that were left in the sink from the night before. Then, I went to my room to do homework.

There wasn't much that first week, but we did have a book to read for English class. The book was titled *Invisible Man* and was written by a black author named Ralph Ellison. Our assignment that night was to read the first twenty-five pages. I highlighted the most interesting parts of those opening pages and noted the words that I didn't recognize so that I could look them up in the dictionary. Just like with any other interesting book from my past, I couldn't put *The Invisible Man* down. There were a lot of different ideas in the book about what it meant to be black. I thought about what that meant for me, coming from Africa to Chicago. In Sudan, I didn't think about what it meant to be black because everyone there was black. In America, things were different. The only black people that I knew in Chicago so far were Miss Grace, Mike and my teammates. The city was black, but my school was not. Miss Grace and Mike seemed like they had a good life. They had work, a place to live and food to eat. But as far as my teammates, the only thing I knew about them was that they didn't seem to take school all that seriously. They were there to play basketball, period.

By midnight, I was on page seventy-five. That's when I closed the book and turned off the light. I put my head out of the window and took a long, deep breath. The air was still warm, but pleasant. I could hear sirens in the distance and the immediate sound of men below talking loudly in front of the building.

I wanted to love Chicago. I saw the buildings downtown, their dark shadows hanging up there over the rest of the city, and I wondered if there were people that looked like me downtown, if warnings about the streets were given there too.

I got into bed and closed my eyes. I let the book soak in. The reason that I couldn't put the book down was because of my connection to the narrator. Like him, I felt invisible. And as I closed my eyes and dozed away, I came to the conclusion that being invisible was part of the reason I made it out of Sudan alive.

After that, I had an easy sleep without any nightmares.

NINE

We talked about *Invisible Man* in English class that day and the teacher asked us what we thought about the roles of young black men in society. That was a strange discussion to be having in our class, because other than Marvin, one or two others, and me, there weren't any black faces. A few of the white students in class had their own views about young black men in America. The teacher, who was also white, shared her own thoughts from time to time. All of the comments during the discussion seemed to lack original thought.

I looked back at Marvin and he was fast asleep.

If there was going to be a black opinion in class, it was going to have to come from me.

I raised my hand and the teacher's eyes lit up with surprise.

"Yes, Serge?" she asked. "What do you have to add?"

"I felt a connection to the narrator in the book," I said. "He was only able to get success after performing for the white people in charge."

I flipped to the early pages in the book.

"Like when he got the college scholarship," I said. "So when we talk about the roles of young black men in society, I think that one has been ignored."

"What role is that?" she asked.

"A young black male, at least in America, sometimes takes on the role of an entertainer."

"Entertainer?" she asked. "Who are they entertaining?"

"Everyone," I said. "I guess, most of all, white people."

The only sound you could hear in the classroom was Marvin snoring in the back.

"That's . . . " she said. "I'm not sure that's appropriate, Serge."

"That's what the story said to me," I said. Now I was feeling slightly embarrassed. "I could be wrong."

"And you haven't told us yet, where your connection to the narrator comes from."

"Well, I'm here on a scholarship to play basketball," I said. "My coach is white. The scout who found me in Africa is white. I wouldn't be here if these people hadn't come into my life."

The room was still silent and the teacher bit down on her lip in silence as well. The moment was uncomfortable, to say the least. I wished I had not spoken.

———

After English class, I met Kyle in the cafeteria.

"Hey Kyle," I said. "What do you think about Chicago?"

"I think it's the best place on earth," he said with a smile. "No, seriously, I think that you couldn't have come to a better city. It's big and the people are friendly, and there's so much to see. Great food, too."

"I want to see some of it," I said. "Other than South Side. That's where I live now."

"Sure," he said. "How about this Saturday? We could meet up and I could take you around to see some of the sights."

"Yes. Saturday."

Some of the guys from the team were sitting together at a lunch table at the far end of the cafeteria. Rodney wasn't with them, and come to think of it, I never saw him during my lunch. He probably had a different lunch period than me. I was glad to have met Kyle. If not for him, I would've eaten alone every day.

I met a woman named Joyce in the Admissions Office after school. She was an older white woman with a gentle smile and soft green eyes. She showed me around the office and let me know that it would just be her and me working together after school.

Learning the phones was first. The most important responsibility here was transferring calls to different faculty mailboxes. Then, it was time to master the photocopier and start on the endless pile of promotional material that the school needed copied. After working for ten minutes I started to actually miss the sugarcane fields.

———

An hour later, I caught up with my team in the weight room for a lower-body lifting session. I had improved to the point that Gene didn't always need to be around when it was my turn to lift. He was free to walk around the room and assist any of the other players. It felt good to gain his trust on that, and so fast. I finished all of my lifts, almost sprinting from rack to rack, and went over to the gym before anyone else. I got up a few jump shots, focusing again on my new form, before practice started.

The rest of the guys joined and we got to work. Rodney nodded to me as we stretched, but didn't say anything. I didn't want to say anything either. I didn't want to seem too eager. I decided to let my game do the talking for me and continue gaining his respect—as well as the respect of the other guys.

We started with defense and it became clear that we were going to be a team that could stop people from scoring. Without counting me, almost all of the other guys on the team had long arms and could jump. Adding me made the team's defense even stronger. I performed well in the rebounding drills again, not allowing a single rebound out of my grasp. During one of the plays, another big guy on the team—Deron—pushed me in my back as I was mid-air going up for a rebound. Even off balance, the ball was still mine. Adding even more insult to Deron, I landed on my feet cleanly. He cursed in my direction under his breath, but I didn't reply.

When it was time for the scrimmage, I played with the starters again. When Coach divided us into teams, a few of the guys rolled their eyes, but I didn't care. I wasn't scared of anybody and didn't want to sell myself short. There was an opportunity to take a starting position. I wasn't going to pass it up. Where I came from, every person fought for what they had in life—every opportunity. Giving in was not an option.

I blocked a shot on the first possession of the scrimmage. On the other end, I finished the sequence with an offensive rebound and a put-back dunk.

"Yeah, Serge!" Coach yelled, clapping his hands. I felt strong *and* light out there. The weight lifting didn't slow me down and my stamina was at its peak, as usual. I didn't want the feeling to go away. It felt like nothing could slow me down.

I blocked two more shots on consecutive possessions—Cornelius on one, Marvin on the other. The next time down, Cornelius gave me a hard elbow to my side as we battled for a rebound. None of the Coaches saw. It stung pretty good and I was sure I'd have a bruise there by morning.

I walked down to the other end, rubbing my side.

"What's wrong?" Coach asked. "You okay?"

"I'm fine," I said, running to join the rest of my teammates.

Coach blew the whistle. "Stop the time!" he called out.

Time stopped ticking away.

"Get some water!" Coach said to us.

He walked over to me.

"What is it, your side?"

"Yeah."

"What happened? Take an elbow?"

I looked over at Cornelius, who was taking a sip of water. He eyed me cautiously as I eyed him back.

"I just pulled it."

"Do you need to come out?"

"No."

"Okay," he said.

I walked over to Rodney and he handed me a water bottle.

"Teams aren't gonna know what to do when they play us," Rodney said.

"What do you mean?"

"You on the defensive end, blocking shots, cleaning the glass," he said. "Me gettin' buckets on the other end."

He shook his head and twisted his mouth.

"Curtains," he said.

I rubbed at my side a few more times and it was fine. I was ready to get right back into it. Cornelius, or anybody else on the team for that matter, wasn't going to push me around. When the clock started again, I blocked another of Cornelius's shots and secured the rebound. I threw a full-court outlet pass to Rodney for a dunk on the other end.

After his feet hit the floor, Rodney looked to me and pointed. I pointed back at him and turned to get into my defensive position. That's when I felt two big hands at my back. They pushed me to the floor and I tumbled. The rest of the guys "oohed," and when I stopped rolling and landed on my back, I looked up to see Cornelius standing over me with a crazed look in his eyes.

"The fuck you doin'? Why you goin' so hard in a fuckin' scrimmage?"

Coach blew the whistle and he and the rest of the guys ran over.

"Better get your ass back to Africa!" he shouted, right before Coach and a few of the guys grabbed him by the shoulders and pulled him back.

There was spit hanging out of his mouth as he

yelled at me. Coach wheeled around and got right in Cornelius's face.

"That's it! Get out of here! Get out of my sight! And don't come back! You're done!"

Cornelius broke his arms free and tears dropped down his face. He left the court with slow, heavy steps.

I got up off the floor and looked at the rest of the team. There was anger in their eyes, but I didn't understand why. I turned to walk away. Rodney grabbed me by the shoulder, turned me around, and brought me back to the team. Coach took a deep breath and looked around at us.

"Okay, huddle up, goddammit," he said between deep breaths.

We circled around. I tried to slow my heavy breathing, but my chest kept filling up.

"I'm not gonna put up with this shit. There will be no jealousy on this team. What I just saw was terrible! Makes me sick!" Coach said. "You guys are supposed to look out for each other. Like family."

He paused for a moment to look around the circle again.

"I don't care if you're new or if you played a big role on the team last year. You have to earn the right to step on the floor. Every time!"

Coach turned to look at me and then back to the whole team.

"I don't want to see something like that ever again," he said. "Get the hell out of here. Hit the showers and think about what happened. Practice is over."

Coach asked Rodney and me to stay behind. When it was just the three of us there, he looked at me and smiled, father-like. "I think you've gotten their attention."

"Coach I don't want to—"

"You don't worry about a thing," he said. "Keep doing what you're doing. We brought you over here because you can play. And what you've shown us here in these first few weeks is that there's no reason to wait. This is Rodney's last year here and we think we can win a city title. You can help us do that."

I didn't say anything, and neither did Rodney.

"They just have to get used to it," he said.

"Okay."

"Go on back there," he said with a nod to the locker room.

I jogged over and turned around to look back at the court before I went inside. Coach was talking and Rodney was nodding his head.

———

I didn't see Cornelius in the locker room. He had already left. The rest of guys were quiet while they changed. There was no rap music, no laughs. I got a couple of cold stares, but let them roll off my back. This was not making any sense to me. What had I done wrong?

Rodney entered, still sweaty in his practice uniform. His eyes held purpose and he walked over to where we all were. He looked around the room and everyone else took notice, stopping what they were doing.

"I need to talk, and you all need to listen."

No one made a sound.

"Where is Cornelius?"

"He rolled out," one of the guys said.

"I'll deal with that nigga later," he said. "The next person who pulls some shit like that is going to have to deal with me, not Coach or the principal. The shit Cornelius pulled on my boy Serge—just tell that fat motherfucka he's gonna have to deal with me."

I knew Rodney was the best player on the team and that everyone respected his skills, but this was something different. This was fear. I knew when I saw it. The rest of the guys feared Rodney.

"You hear?" he yelled. "We ain't gonna be about that. That ain't gonna be us."

He looked around the room one last time and was done. He went to his locker, grabbed a towel, and walked over to the showers. The room relaxed a little when he left, but not by much. The guys still didn't talk.

I looked around and no one else looked back at me. I sat down in front of my locker and felt the sweat bead on my forehead. I wiped it with a towel and sighed deeply. I looked up again and the locker room was empty. I was the only one left inside.

I took my bags and left the locker room.

The bus came and I paid the dollar to get on. It felt good to have money in my pocket. I couldn't wait to pay Miss Grace back.

TEN

"**W**e missed you last night," Miss Grace said with her wide smile as she broke green beans in half. "We saw the light on in your room, but we didn't want to bother you."

"I wanted to thank you for the food. It was delicious. All of your food is."

"Aw, don't mention it," she said. "I'm glad you enjoy it."

I told Miss Grace about my job at school, and she smiled proudly, as if I was her own child.

There was still about an hour before dinner. That gave me time to work on some homework.

I did my math homework quickly and easily. It

helped that Mr. Sesay took the time to explain the concepts all the way through.

The only other assignment for the night was in English class, a writing assignment that asked us "to describe a situation or time in your life when you felt like an invisible man."

I thought about the times when I felt invisible, and at first they were too many to count. In Sudan, growing up with my dad and Sefu, that feeling was always there—the feeling of being overlooked. It wasn't until basketball came into my life that I felt like I even *had* a life of my own.

It was clear to me that my father favored Sefu for the simple fact that he was his oldest son. I never said anything to him about it because conversations like that were unheard of in Sudan.

Maybe that's why basketball became such a big thing in my life. At first, I didn't see it as a way out of Africa. I played the game because it made me feel good. Once I stopped going to school to help my dad on the farm, there weren't a lot of moments where I felt good about myself. We were poor, but that wasn't it. There was always food on our table, clothes on our backs, and a roof over our heads. I needed something that was just for me. I needed it just like I needed air. And basketball—the basketball court—was the only thing, the only place in Sudan that I could breathe. It was the only place that I could get air.

As I grew as a player, and possibilities in my life opened up, I became more invisible in the eyes of my father and Sefu. It hurt that they weren't proud of me, that they didn't support me like my mother had. One day, a very hot day in the fields, my father lashed out at me and said that a man's first responsibility is to take care of his family, not play some silly game. Sefu just added to it with his silence and that cold stare that he had inherited from our father.

I told them that day in the fields that I wanted to get out of Africa, out of Sudan, because it was suffocating me. They were suffocating me. My father called me a disgrace.

We didn't speak for a few days and I left for a tournament in another part of southern Sudan without saying goodbye to my father and Sefu. When I got back, I was up early to work on the farm. They didn't say a word to me on those walks to and from the farm. They didn't ask about the tournament or even how I played.

I felt invisible again and again, each morning and night. And then during one of those black nights, I knew. I had to get out. I didn't want to feel that way ever again.

Miss Grace knocked on the door.

"Serge," she said, "dinner's ready."

I stopped writing and looked up at her.

"I'll be right out."

I finished a sentence and the assignment was done, or at least I thought it was done. After dinner, I sat with Mike in the living room and we watched a Chicago Bulls preseason game in which Derrick Rose scored thirty-nine points.

I went back into my room and got into bed. The nightmares stayed away for another night.

ELEVEN

"That's great," Miss Grace said after breakfast the next morning. "You already have a friend from school."

"He's very nice." I said.

On my fourth Saturday in Chicago, I didn't have practice. Kyle and I arranged to meet on Lakeshore Drive. My tour of Chicago would start at Grant Park.

"You have to walk up a few blocks on Halstead," she said, pointing out the window, "and catch the downtown train. When you get to Grant Park, you won't miss it because that's where everyone will be getting off."

"Thanks, Miss Grace."

I gathered a few things in my book bag, including a bottle of water and a few energy bars from the training room at school. It was a hot day, so there was no need for a jacket or sweater. What my bag missed was a camera to take pictures of the city. As soon as I saved enough money, I'd get one.

I left the apartment and walked the few blocks up Halstead to the train station. There were some people standing outside of the station asking for money. Most people just ignored them, acting as if they weren't even there, while a few complained out loud about their presence. I just put my head down and walked past them and into the terminal. I bought a one-way ticket downtown with the help of a security guard inside the station. He commented on my height and asked if I played ball. I nodded "yes" and he wished me luck during the season.

I took the stairs down to the platform and there was a train with open doors waiting to leave. I hurried over to catch it, and when I got inside, the car was nearly half-full. I walked past a few empty seats and found a spot near a window where I could stand.

I didn't realize how big the city of Chicago was until the train exited the tunnel and reached higher ground. The sky was a clear and crystal blue, and the tall buildings of downtown rested perfectly against it. The sun was high. The buildings sparkled. The car filled up a little more with every stop. People rushed in and grabbed seats when they could, settling for spots to stand when they had to. The crowd didn't bother me any. Because of my height, I could comfortably look out the window and take in the sights. Besides, the buses in Sudan were twice as crowded—and the crowds often included animals and cargo.

As we got closer to downtown, the train filled up to its maximum. There was a mix of white, black, and every kind of face you could imagine. Many of them had cameras hanging off their necks.

There was an excitement in the train. People had places to be. They checked their watches, looked at their phones, and stared ahead in a very American way. They were focused on what was next, be it school, or work, or play. There was plenty of light left in the day for whatever they were after.

There was a bend in the tracks and the train slightly changed course. Out of nowhere came the massive body of water called Lake Michigan. It was as if it appeared out of thin air. My eyes stayed glued to the shimmering expanse as the train rumbled onto a straight path again for several minutes. Then a voice overhead called out, "Grant Park!" as the next stop neared, and everyone on the train shuffled in anticipation to depart.

The metallic wheels of the train groaned to a stop. I couldn't wait to get out and explore this new place, my new city.

On school days, I had a routine and it left no room to diverge. I decided that from now on, the weekends would be my time to explore. At least before the season started, anyway.

I exited the station and followed the crowd through a tunneled pathway. We walked for a few blocks until I noticed a massive structure with columns, and in its center, there was a huge field of green grass. The structure was called "Soldier Field," the place where Mike's both beloved and hated Chicago Bears played their games.

Kyle and I planned to meet at the Buckingham Fountain. I didn't need to ask where it was because, as I followed the other passengers off the train and into Grant Park, the fountain stood right in the center. Lots of people were hanging around the fountain. Kyle and I weren't the only ones using it as a meeting place. People of all different colors, shapes, and sizes were there taking pictures, shaking hands, and hugging. I thought how nice it would be to get comfortable in Chicago, comfortable enough to walk around the streets without feeling like an outsider. Maybe I'd even get comfortable enough to meet a girl. This was a good first step though.

I wasn't afraid to leave the comfort zone that I had at school and with basketball. I wanted to meet others and talk about books and other interesting things. I didn't want to *talk* about basketball. I was a basketball player. But that's not all I was. I wanted to be more than just a basketball player. And from the looks of all the people, with their wide smiles and open arms, Chicago would be the place for me to achieve that. It was a place where I could be anything I wanted. I was in America and for the first time I wanted to be an American.

I looked around for Kyle and didn't see him. I wiped some sweat from my forehead and looked up to the yellow disc in the sky. It was a hot day, but the lack of humidity made it bearable. The heat I had grown up with was much more dramatic.

The breathtaking view of the downtown skyscrapers in front of a cloudless sky put me in a quick trance that was broken by the group of girls screaming and giggling right next to me. There were a lot of people out that day. It felt good to be free and kind of, well, accepted. No one looked at me funny because my skin was dark or because I was much taller than everyone else. It was funny, I felt more secure in Chicago than I ever did in Sudan. Maybe it was just the sensation of being in a new place. Whatever it was, I liked the feeling.

"Hey Serge!" I heard, from behind.

I turned around and saw Kyle walking over to me. He was wearing a pair of blue jeans and a red Chicago Bulls T-shirt.

"What's up, Kyle?" I said, as I approached him. We shook hands.

"Sorry I'm a little late," he said. "The cab driver took a wrong turn and we hit a bunch of traffic."

"It's okay," I said. "I've been enjoying this."

I waved a hand to Lake Michigan.

We started by walking around Grant Park. Kyle stopped at different places to point out the name and origins of the things we passed. When he spoke, the feeling was natural and the enjoyment on his face was pure.

"You really like helping people, don't you?" I asked, as we walked through the huge park.

"Yeah," he said. "I do. I love the city and our school and it just makes me feel good."

"Where do you think you got it from? The interest in helping people?" I asked.

"My parents," he said, before walking a little ahead of me, then a little faster.

Right away I thought of my mother, my father, and my brothers and sisters. I forced a smile.

We made our way over to Millennium Park. Kyle was silent now, but this place didn't need any explanation. All you needed here were your eyes. The Cloud Gate was the first sculpture we approached. Kyle said that no one in Chicago called it that; they simply called it "The Bean" because of its shape. The Bean was made of some kind of reflective metal and I studied my reflection in it while people's reflections danced and wobbled behind me.

We then made our way over to Wrigley Square, and as we got closer to it, columns stretched up to form an arch. Kyle's eyes lit up as if he were looking at it for the first time.

"It looks like something that you would see in Ancient Rome," I said.

Kyle smiled and continued walking towards the columns.

"It's the Millennium Monument," he said.

We stopped on the lawn directly in front of the monument and gazed up at the columns. There was a perfect backdrop of the city behind it, with one skyscraper shooting through the top of the arch. We sat down on the lawn and there were others around doing the same. It was a nice view and it felt like a place where people came to relax in the shadow of something ancient.

"Used to come here all the time, Serge," Kyle said.

"You haven't been here lately?" I asked.

He shook his head. "Nope."

"How come?"

"Like I said, for a while this was the place," he said. "My parents and I used to walk here all the time in the spring and summers. When the weather was really good, we'd stay all day, have picnics and stuff."

I stayed silent.

"But after that, there wasn't much reason to come back here," he said, "until today."

There was another fountain right in front of the columns. Kids were playing near the water as their parents sat nearby. It was a peaceful place and I could see why Kyle and his parents liked it so much.

"Ready to see some more?" Kyle asked.

"Sure."

We walked in silence over to the Jay Pritzker

Pavilion. It was an odd-looking silver structure, with arms of metal that stretched and snaked over an open, green field. People sat alone and in groups on the grass here too. I heard so many different languages being spoken—it was exciting. Being from Sudan was no big deal for a few moments.

Kyle and I walked closer to the structure. It was then, and only then, that I realized what the purpose of this strange thing was. It was a place where concerts were held, and from what I could tell, people would stand on the field and look to the stage inside the metal shell. There was nothing like that in Darfur.

I looked over to Kyle as he looked up to the ceiling of the pavilion. There was some kind of hurt in his eyes. As someone who had plenty of hurt in his—I just knew.

"Weird isn't it?" he asked.

"Yes."

"Have you even been to a concert?" he asked.

"No," I said. "Have you?"

"Yeah," he said. "This is one of the most interesting places to see live music in Chicago, especially at night and in the summer. The sun goes down and the lights go on. The buildings fade out in the background."

"What makes it so interesting, other than the way it looks?" I asked.

"I don't know," he said. "It's like you're here listening to a band play. Or I remember this one time when my mom brought me here to see a string quartet in concert—you know, like symphony music—and at first, I didn't want to come because I didn't think I'd like that kind of music. But when we got here and I saw all the people, when the sun went down and the music started . . . "

He paused for a moment and looked down to the grass. A bead of sweat dripped down his forehead. He looked up to me.

"Something magical happened."

"Was the music good?" I asked with a smile.

He smiled back.

"It was. But it was all of that stuff mixed together," he said. "I'll never forget that night."

We were both quiet for a moment.

"More?" he asked.

"Yeah."

"You're not tired and hot yet?" he asked.

"This isn't tiring for me. And this weather, this is nothing," I said. "In Sudan, it can be much hotter." I almost continued this thought. *And my family and I worked in the sugarcane fields into the night. And I was tired. And my brother and father were killed.* But I didn't speak these words. I wasn't ready to.

The last sculpture we walked to was the Crown Fountain. There were people cooling themselves in the water that spurt out of a black girl's face painted on the side of the sculpture. Kyle was quiet once again as we looked at the crowd of people around the sculpture. I walked closer to it, leaving him behind. He didn't seem to mind because he smiled when I walked ahead. When I got up there,

I realized that the girl's face wasn't painted on. It was a television screen that produced the image of a black female face with cold water shooting out of a hole in the screen where her mouth was. As a piece of art, I didn't understand it. But on hot days like this one, the cold water made sense.

I reached over a few kids and stuck my hand out to feel the water. It was ice cold. I pulled it back quickly and after taking a few steps back, another group of small kids took my place right next to the screen. I walked back over to Kyle.

"I didn't know it was going to be that cold," I said.

"It's crazy isn't it?" he asked. "How much water we waste here."

"Yeah, you wouldn't see this where I come from. Water is like gold."

There was more silence, and this time I saw a streak of anger on Kyle's face. His behavior was a bit confusing—switching between happiness, sadness, and anger, but I didn't mind. He was my friend—and I understood the ups and downs deep pain can cause.

"You hungry?" he asked.

I nodded.

"'Let's get a Chicago dog."

"A dog?" I asked.

"A hot dog—its not a real dog. Don't worry," he laughed.

We walked over to a stand and got in line. Kyle ordered two "Chicago dogs" and two sodas. We took the food over to a bench and sat while we ate. The messy "Chicago Dog" was tasty and spicy. I loved it.

"Who thought to put all of these ingredients on this?" I asked before taking my last bite.

"I don't know," he said. "But it tastes good."

He finished his and sat quietly for a moment.

"Hey," he said. "What was it like? Living in Sudan? I've read a lot about the genocide. But I want to know about the day-to-day life there."

"Life is hard," I said. "Many people don't have

the chance to live in peace because of the rebels. People are poor, too. That gives the rebels another weapon."

Kyle shook his head.

"Why are you interested in Sudan?"

"I spent some time in Africa," he said. "My parents and I lived in Kenya for three years."

"You lived in Kenya?"

"My parents were stationed there. They worked for the United Nations."

I knew the United Nations from Sudan.

"When did you and your parents return to the States?"

"They never returned."

"Are they still there?"

"No," he said. "They died there."

Kyle paused and I could see the damage done by just saying the words. My stomach curdled and I felt bad because I had no words for him. There were no words for what he was feeling.

I knew.

"They were shot and killed in a shopping mall," he said after another long period of silence. "Rebels."

And suddenly, Kyle's reading on the rebels of Sudan made sense. His interest in me made sense. It all did.

I didn't say anything for a long time after. We sat on the bench for fifteen more minutes or so, looking at the people smiling as they snapped pictures of Crown Fountain while others enjoyed their Chicago Dogs.

"Let's get out of here, Serge," Kyle said abruptly. "I want to show you something."

———

Kyle called for a taxi. We got in and headed for a different part of the city. He told the driver where to go then leaned back in his seat next to mine. The ride took twenty minutes and most of that seemed to be because of the traffic. During the ride, I looked out of the window and stared straight up. The tops of the old buildings were invisible.

We reached our destination—a place called Burnham Park. We got out of the taxi and Kyle paid the driver with a twenty-dollar bill. His wallet had many more bills in it.

Kyle nodded to something ahead of us as we walked into the park. I could hear voices of young people and the sounds of something like wood scraping against rock. We got closer and I saw where the sounds were coming from. There was a vast pit made out of what looked like a sandy rock. There were some boys skateboarding in and out of the pit. They looked like they were our age, maybe even a little older.

"What is this?"

"A skate park," Kyle said.

We took a walkway to the top of the pit. I stood at the lip of one of the drops and there was a skateboarder in action at the bottom. He gained speed and jumped up on the lip of the other side directly across from us.

When the skateboarder saw us from across the pit, he smiled and made some kind of hand gesture with his thumb and pinky.

"Kyle!" he said. "What's happening, bro?"

Then there was a strange smell in the air and it was all around us. It was a burning smell, sharp, and it stung my nose. I held my nose because it was so pungent and raw.

Kyle's friend from the other side of the pit got back onto his skateboard and dropped into the hole again. He gained speed and reached us.

They shook hands and Kyle turned to me.

"Steve, this is my pal Serge from school," he said. "He's from Sudan. And he plays ball."

"Great to meet you, Serge," Steve said as we shook. "You're from Sudan, huh? Some fucked up shit going on down there, huh?"

I nodded and sniffed at the air again.

"You guys wanna go spark one?" Steve asked as

he started toward the walkway that we had taken to get to the top of the pit.

We followed him down the walkway and through the park into a wooded area where the burnt smell was even stronger. There were other people there, too, smoking thin cigarettes and drinking beer from cans.

Kyle looked up at me.

"Have you ever smoked pot before?"

"Pot?"

"Marijuana?"

I shook my head.

Steve introduced us to the others. They looked relaxed and carried smiles on their faces as they shook our hands.

Everyone stood in a circle now. Steve lit one of the thin cigarettes. After he was finished taking a few puffs off of it, he passed it to the person to his right, and when that person was done, he did the same. When it got to Kyle, he looked at me before taking a puff. His face, too, became relaxed, and then adopted the same lazy, smiling expression as everyone else in the woods. He held the cigarette out to me, its edges burning while the smoke swirled up into the air. I waved it off. He reached in front of me and passed it to the person on my right.

The thin cigarette went around the circle three times before it was tossed away. I didn't take one puff, but I didn't leave the woods either.

———

We were out of the woods again near the skate park. Some of the people from the woods were skating inside of the park and some were sitting on the grass that surrounded it.

Steve, Kyle, and I were sitting on the grass as the sounds of skateboards crashing on concrete were all around us.

"It helps me, you know?" Kyle said. "Helps with the pain."

"Do you have any brothers or sisters?" I asked.

"Nope," he said. "Just me."

He looked straight-ahead and then up into the orange sky. The sun was starting to fall. I could understand his pain. He didn't owe me any explanations. I was his friend and there to help him if I could. It struck me that the world was a small place. Kyle and I had something in common that was unthinkable—we both had family members that were shot and killed in Africa. How strange.

"If you don't mind me asking," I said, "were you in Africa at the time that they were killed?"

"No," he said. "I was here. It was in the summer when it happened. Over the years, no matter where we lived in the world—Kenya, Philippines, Rome—I always spent my summers here with my aunt. My parents were getting ready to come here that summer as well. I came ahead of them by a couple of weeks because my school in Kenya was finished for the year and I wanted to go to this summer basketball camp at DePaul."

I didn't say anything.

"I got the news while I was in camp."

There was more silence after that. I was honored that, even though we were friends for just a little while, Kyle shared the story of his parents with me. I wasn't sure if I wanted to share my similar story with him, though. I didn't think it was the right time.

I just sat there with him until he was ready to leave. The skate park, with its unusual tribesmen, was a place that Kyle felt safe. It was a place that he came to relieve the pain. I sat there and felt very peaceful. I understood why Kyle liked it here.

TWELVE

The sun had set when we got into another cab outside of Burnham Park. Kyle insisted on having the cab take me all the way to Miss Grace's apartment.

Kyle told the cab driver to take "the long way" to South Side, along Lakeshore drive. The windows were down in the cab and the air was still warm as we drove next to the massive, now black, body of water. The breeze was pleasant. Combined with the lights of downtown, it made for a nice view.

We didn't say much on the ride home. Kyle closed his eyes as the breeze blew into his face.

I was tired, both physically and mentally. I wanted to close my eyes, but I was afraid that the nightmares would come back.

I kept them open until we reached Miss Grace's apartment. I tapped Kyle on the shoulder when the cab driver stopped out front.

"Thanks for showing me around Chicago," I said. "And also for the ride. You didn't have to pay my way but I thank you."

"Don't mention it," he said, blinking his eyes a few times. "Hey man, I'm sorry that I kind of took over the day. I was supposed to show you more things around the city. Instead, you spent most of your time at a skate park listening to . . . "

I cut him off, "It's okay," I said. "There will be plenty of time to see the city. Thank you for telling me about your life. I am honored."

He smiled for the first time in hours.

"You're a good guy, Serge," he said. "I'm glad we bumped into each other that day in the halls."

"Me too," I said. "It was lucky for me."

A couple of guys walked past the cab on the sidewalk. They stared into the cab while they went by.

I opened the door of the cab. Kyle and I bumped fists and I got out.

The cab pulled away and I walked toward Miss Grace's apartment building. My mouth was dry and I remembered that the corner store down a couple of blocks on Halstead had the flavor of Gatorade that I loved. I turned around, walked down Halstead, and went into the store. The clerk was a brown-skinned man who acknowledged me with a nod. There was no one else in the store. I picked out the Gatorade from the refrigerated case and made my way up to the clerk.

When I got near the cash register, the front door burst open and two men wearing all black and black masks rushed in. They went straight to the front where I stood and both of them had guns.

"You know what the fuck this is!" one of them

screamed. He held his gun firmly with two hands and pointed it at the clerk.

"Empty the register!" he said. "And hurry up. Don't make me act crazy up in here!"

The other one was next to me, pointing his gun into my side. I stood very still.

"Whatchu got, big man?" he asked me in a calm voice, waving his gun at the pocket that held my money.

I reached into my pocket and gave him the little money I had—about twelve dollars.

"You're wasting my fuckin' time!" the first one said.

I closed my eyes and dropped to the floor. Suddenly, I was back in Sudan in the brush with my father and Sefu, close enough to hear, but not touch.

The clerk didn't say anything and when the gunman repeated his directions, I heard the cash register finally open.

"That's better," the first one said. "Now I know you got some more cheese in the back."

There were sirens in the distance. I opened my eyes. The gunman shifted his feet and then unleashed two shots at the clerk. I hit the floor and went face down on the tile, closing my eyes again. There was another shot. And another. I heard the clerk's body smash into the cigarette racks behind the register.

The two men with guns ran out of the store. The sirens were getting closer. From the sound of the shots, the clerk didn't have a chance. After a few more moments on the floor, the sounds of the sirens slipped out of my mind and the only thing I *could* hear in the store was the sound of my heavy breathing. I slowly got up off the floor and my legs wobbled. I steadied myself on a rack behind me. The sirens came back, and with them, the sounds of tires screeching to a halt in front the store. The flashes of red and blue reflected off the windows in the front. I walked to where the clerk was and leaned my head over the counter. His body was torn apart and sprawled out in a pool of slick red underneath the cigarette racks. His eyes were still open and foggy. They were staring past me. Now I had two nightmares to worry about.

THIRTEEN

After the shots, I was frozen in the woods. The moon was high and clear, and the silence after the mayhem chilled the cool desert air. I could hear the laughs of the men who killed my father and Sefu. They were coming close. It was just a matter of time before they got me, too. When these men came to kill, everyone had to die. No one was spared, not even women and children.

Sitting there, I wasn't ready to die. But it was out of my hands. I held my breath and waited for it. I imagined what it would feel like when the hot bullets ripped through my flesh.

I didn't go to school for a few days after the corner store shooting. The nightmares came back to me every night and they were worse than before. I didn't know what to do, and because I wasn't getting any sleep, I couldn't get out of bed.

Miss Grace and Mike didn't mind that I stayed home from school. Their biggest concern was that I wasn't leaving my room, not even to eat. Miss Grace would bring food to my room, and because I wanted to be polite, I accepted it. I never took more than a few bites, though.

Coach, too, said it was okay to take some time away from school and basketball. He understood that it wasn't easy for me to deal with what happened, especially with my past. Luol Deng called me as well to make sure I was okay. I told him that I would survive, but deep down inside I wasn't really sure. I wondered *why* were there people in the world who were so willing to kill.

I couldn't read. I couldn't do any of the homework that my teachers sent home. I couldn't do anything. The images of death followed me wherever I went. Bodies shredded by bullets flooded whichever place my mind drifted to. I thought I had escaped the violence when I left Sudan, but I was wrong. Chicago had its own problems.

———

When it was time to go back to school on the following Monday, I didn't resist.

I walked out to the living room after showering and changing into my school uniform. I was dressed and carrying my book bag and gym bag. I caught my reflection in a mirror that hung on the wall next to the framed pictures. I looked tired. My eyes were dead with no hope of changing into something more inspiring. I *looked* like the student-athlete I was before the shooting at the corner store, but I was him in looks only. Part of my spirit had been taken away from me that night, and I wasn't sure that I had the strength to get it back.

Miss Grace walked out of the kitchen just then with a plate of breakfast. I barely ate.

"Hi Serge," she said. "How are you?"

"Hello, Miss Grace."

I put my two bags down next to the couch.

"Do you think you're ready to go back to school? Ready to get back out there on that court?"

I put my head down and took in a deep breath through my mouth. My eyes started to water. She put her hand at my back and pulled me in for a hug. I put my arms around her and squeezed her tight, realizing that I missed my own mother.

I pulled away from Miss Grace and wiped the tears with my sleeve.

"I'm here if you need someone to talk to," she said. "Mike, too."

"It's okay," I said. "I have to go."

I picked up my bags and walked out of the door.

The air was cooler outside as we were now getting close to fall. I didn't know exactly what that meant for Chicago, but from what everyone had told me, the fall months were to be enjoyed because they were the last months of decent weather until spring.

I got to school not knowing how I'd react. I also didn't know if the other students knew the real reason for my weeklong absence. That made me even more anxious. I didn't want unnecessary attention or pity for what had happened.

The first few classes went by and I didn't participate like I normally did. I listened in class to what my teachers were saying as much as I could, but didn't do much else. It was a big effort not to let my mind drift, an effort that I wasn't up for. The guys on the team didn't say anything to me. They just watched me as I walked by in the halls or, in Marvin's case, the classroom. I didn't see Kyle or Rodney, my only two friends in Chicago, that day.

After lunch, when I walked into Mr. Sesay's class and sat down, he came over to my desk. He put his hand on my shoulder and leaned in close. "Serge," he said quietly. "I heard what happened. I called your host mother, Miss Grace, to try to come see you. But she said you didn't want to see anyone."

I smiled dreamily. "Thanks for calling."

"I'm so sorry," he said.

"You don't have to be sorry, Mr. Sesay," I said. "You didn't do anything."

He looked past me for a moment as the seats in class began filling up behind me.

"Listen, I want you to come talk to me after school," he said.

I had practice after school, but I could be a little late. Coach would understand.

"Okay," I said.

"Right after school, I'll be here," he said.

———

"Okay," Mr. Sesay said in his empty classroom after school had ended, "what happened that night?"

"I went to the store to get a drink and right as I'm about to pay, these two men dressed in black came into the store to rob it. One of them had a gun—a big gun—pointed at the clerk. The other came close and pointed a smaller gun at me."

"And then what happened?"

"It was going smoothly, I guess. The clerk opened the register—I heard it—and started gathering the money. But then the police sirens started getting closer, and the one with the big gun just shot the clerk."

Mr. Sesay shook his head.

"I know it's hard, Serge," he said. "But every day it will get a little bit better. The pain will go down a little more."

"I've already been through this," I said. "That's the problem."

"What do you mean?"

"My father and brother were shot by rebels back

in Darfur a little over a year ago. They died. Being in that store, it was like—"

The words still felt strange coming out of my mouth.

"Reliving your past," he said.

"Yes. I just don't know if I am going to be able to get over this," I said. "With my father and brother, I didn't see them killed. I *heard* it. There are no specific images of their dead bodies in my head. Now I can clearly imagine . . . " I paused, fighting back tears, "I can imagine what their bodies looked like after they were killed. I keep picturing my father and brother dead, but staring at me with open eyes. There's no safety for me. When I sleep, I see the bloody bodies of my father and brother, and when I'm awake, I think about the clerk."

Mr. Sesay thought for a moment. His face finally softened and he smiled.

"You have to keep going," he said. "Life is hard where we come from. Life is hard here in Chicago. But you made it here. And you have talent along with brains. You can do something special with your life."

A tear fell down the side of my face and I bowed my head.

"You have to keep going, though," he said. "It's the only way. Only the strong survive. Are you strong enough, Serge?"

FOURTEEN

In the weeks after the shooting, I tried to bury myself in a routine: school, work, basketball. Two detectives from the Chicago police department talked to me. They wanted to know if I could identify the shooters. I told them about the masks and guns—the big one and the smaller one. I told them that one of the guys was shouting while the other one was calm.

Another week or two passed and the police stopped bothering me, stopped coming by the apartment. Miss Grace said that the clerk's murder would go unsolved, that there were too many murders to solve.

The nightmares came and went and I still wasn't sleeping much, if any at all. I got accustomed to not getting much sleep. Sometimes I stayed wide-awake during the nights without nightmares.

With all that time to think, my thoughts often went to my father and Sefu. I focused on the final moment of their lives. The shouting. The gunshots. A tremendous feeling of guilt descended on me. And all of a sudden, I couldn't forgive myself for leaving Sudan after their deaths—for leaving my mother.

Concentrating in school became impossible. I was too distracted, too sad. I wasn't as excited about the reading in English class as I was before the incident. I felt like I couldn't breathe. I felt like the invisible man again.

I thought about the question Mr. Sesay had asked me: *Are you strong enough, Serge?* The answer was no.

A few weeks after the shooting, I was in the Admissions Office for work. Because it was a slow day—no calls coming in, no pamphlets to copy—I picked up a newspaper that was lying around and read the front page. There was an article about how Chicago had five hundred murders for the year. That number didn't mean much to me because I was from a place where five hundred murders was surpassed in six months, maybe even faster, depending on if there was a particularly brutal rebel group on a killing spree. To the writer of the article, though, five hundred was a shocking number—even for Chicago. Guns were the problem, the writer said, the *only* problem. But I wasn't so sure that was true. The writer of the article was missing something, something that Miss Grace had mentioned when I first moved to Chicago. The anger.

The article said nothing about the anger of the people who were committing the murders.

I thought about how angry you had to be to kill a man with a gun.

I thought about the angry men in Sudan, the angry men who shot my father and Sefu.

Angry about what?

I didn't know. But what I did know was that nothing was being done about it.

I folded the newspaper and realized that Chicago and Sudan were the same place.

———

The only thing that *was* working out for me was basketball. That was a surprise, considering the rest of my life was falling apart. I had managed to keep my spot in the starting lineup. I worked out as hard as I could in the weight room and stayed for extra practice on the court. I don't know where I got the energy from considering all of the sleepless nights.

As the calendar turned from October to November and the temperature cooled quickly, preseason workouts became a thing of the past. It was time for the regular season. You could feel that the intensity had risen in the halls, in the locker room, and on the court.

Coach brought us up in the middle of the weight room, after our last lift of the preseason. He looked around at the group before he spoke. No one said anything as they stared back at him.

"As you all know, tomorrow is the first official day of the season," Coach said, "and we'll have our first practice after school."

It was odd to hear it so quiet in there, without the usual sounds of weight clanging and teammates yelling to each other.

"For the new guys," he said, "we don't play for district titles here." Coach looked right at me.

"We play for city championships."

I looked to Rodney at my right, and he was looking straight ahead at Coach.

That was my first experience with having expectations in my life. I was used to having no expectations at all. I didn't need the extra pressure, especially right then. But Coach's words told me that I would not be able to escape the expectations, even if I tried.

———

It was the Saturday before our first game of the season. That game would be two nights later, on Monday, against a team from New York City. The school had a yearly tradition, which was held after the Saturday practice before the first game. That tradition was "Family Day."

I warmed up by myself down on one end of the court. My teammates were down on the other end and most had at least one of their parents on the court with them. There wasn't much use to me warming up; I wasn't focused at all. Instead, I thought about my mother and siblings back in Darfur. I hadn't talked to my mother since I left and wasn't sure where her and my siblings were living at that time. Because of the incident with my father and Sefu, my mother and siblings—and me too, when I still lived there—had to move from village to village constantly for fear of being harassed, or worse, killed.

I worried most about my mother and sisters. There was a lot of trouble with rape in Darfur, and women and girls there were rarely spared, no matter what their age was.

I missed six straight jump shots before Coach whistled for me to join the rest of the team at midcourt.

"Okay," he said. "This is a tradition here. Some of you guys have experienced it before. For the new guys, this day is to let you know that we are a family. We look out for each other, not only on the court, but also outside these walls."

I looked around the gym and it was the most crowded I had ever seen it. The stands were completely filled. Fathers smiled down on their sons while a group of the mothers set up food tables in the corner of the gym for the party after practice.

"You play for each other and your family, not

just yourselves," he said. "This will be a long year, and we'll fall down along the way. But if we stay together and treat each other with respect," Coach looked at me, "we can take on any challenge. But we do it together."

I looked over to the stands again and then over to the mothers. I put my head down and closed my eyes.

"Ok gentleman," Coach said. "Let's get after it."

I started practice slowly and my energy was way down. My feet were slow as we worked on defense and my box outs were weak during rebounding drills. When it came time for shooting, I didn't have any lift on my jump shot. I didn't make one shot out of ten. I stepped off the court while all my teammates were still practicing. I thought about giving up right then. I didn't think I was strong enough to handle it all: my father and Sefu's death, being alone in America, the violence that seemed to follow me at every turn. *Are you strong enough, Serge?* No. I am not.

Coach walked over to me on the sidelines. He didn't say anything to me at first. He just stood next to me as we both observed the team. The action on the floor never stopped. I don't even think they realized that I was off to the side. The gym was filled with the excitement of a new season. And I had to decide if I wanted to—or if I was even able to—be a part of that excitement.

"I know today is hard for you," Coach said.

"I am sorry for playing badly, Coach," I said. "I'm tired."

"You're not sleeping, are you? I can see the bags under those eyes."

I shook my head and put my hands on my knees.

"I want to keep going. I know that's what I'm supposed to do," I said, "but . . . "

"But you want to leave?"

"I don't know."

He crossed his arms, leaned back, and spread his legs shoulder width apart.

"What I tell you isn't gonna matter, Serge. You have the heart. There's no question about that. You leaving Africa and coming here to chase a dream," he said, "that is brave. That is heart. You are a strong young man. But you have to realize that sometimes it's about doing something that's bigger than yourself. I mean, this is bigger than basketball."

I smiled. "I didn't even know what the game was until I was thirteen."

"We have a lot of problems in this city, Serge," he said. "And I'm sorry about what happened to your family back in Sudan. And I'm sorry about what you had to see in that corner store on Halstead. But the one thing I don't want you to do—the thing I never want you to do—is to think that you are not tough enough for this."

I stared at him and all of the movements and sounds in the gym just went away.

"You're tough," he said. "It doesn't matter if

you ever step on that court again. You made it, Serge. Look around you."

I looked at my teammates running up and down that floor, exploding into the air, doing things that most people only dreamed of. It took a lot of work to gain their respect. No one questioned my ability anymore. No one had a problem with how hard I went anymore. I had earned the team's respect. I was one of them. In all of my sadness, I had failed to notice that accomplishment.

The game of basketball loved me because I was willing to work to get better.

The question was: how much did I love the game?

After a break in practice, I rejoined my teammates for the final part of it, the scrimmage—starters versus reserves. Coach didn't say anything to me. He just motioned for me to take my spot with the starting lineup. Rodney walked over and we pounded fists. He also didn't say anything.

I started the scrimmage much like I had started

practice. I missed a defensive rotation on the first possession, and as a result, the other side got a wide-open three. Our first possession on offense was no better; I didn't move without the ball and that left Rodney no room to operate. He had to force a bad shot, which the other side rebounded.

When the reserves' point guard drove past his man and into the lane, I went for a wild block attempt that left the offensive glass wide open. My man slipped inside and slammed home the missed shot.

After the first part of the scrimmage, we were losing to the reserves twenty-five to eleven. It wasn't a good sign to be losing by that much to our second stringers when we had nationally ranked opponents coming in for the first game of the season.

Rodney approached me on the sidelines during our water break.

"What's up?" he asked.

"I'm alright."

"You're head ain't right."

"I'll be fine."

"Well, are you hurt or something?"

"No."

"You know better than anyone on this team that you gotta fly around when you step on that court," he said. "'Cause if you don't, you ain't shit."

The buzzer sounded. Coach put twelve more minutes up on the clock for the second part of the scrimmage. I had twelve minutes to figure out if I was going to be a part of something bigger.

Rodney stole a pass on the first possession and I sprinted as fast as I could to join him on the break. He saw me streaking down the left side and tossed the ball into the air. I wasn't sure that I could get to it, but my feet left the ground anyway. I saw the ball coming my way and it was a little behind me. I reached far back with my right hand and the ball stuck to the ends of my fingertips. I threw down a powerful, one-handed dunk. I screamed. It was a loud scream. I was screaming to release some of the pain inside me. The scream echoed and the gym erupted. Rodney's eyes lit up as we ran back down on defense.

That *one* play energized me and I began feeling like myself again. All it took was one play. Everyone in the gym saw it. My teammates knew and so did Coach. They could rely on me to give everything I had.

On defense, I controlled the paint and helped out on the perimeter. After one of my six blocks during the second part of the scrimmage, Rodney took the ball and brought it down the floor. I set a screen for him at the top right elbow and rolled to the open space fifteen feet away from the hoop. When the double-team came, Rodney threaded a bounce pass to me with his left hand. With a defender running right at me, I faked the jumper, took two dribbles, and threw down another thunderous, one-handed dunk.

The score was tied at forty with only a minute left to go in the scrimmage. The reserves had the ball. Rodney was beat on defense; his man went by him because he went for a steal and missed it. Our whole defense was unbalanced. I moved my feet as fast as I could to cut Rodney's man off, and when I did, he threw a pass behind me to the player that I was guarding in the paint. The only way that we were going to stop them from scoring was if Rodney raced back to cover my man for me. That's the kind of trust you need out there on the court. I had Rodney's back when he was beaten, and now, he had mine.

By the time my guy received the pass and went up for the score, Rodney flew in from behind to get a hand on the shot. The ball was loose, hanging in the air, and it was free to anyone who wanted it. I jumped as high as I could to grab the ball over three other players. I secured it with both hands.

The starters had the ball with a chance to win the game.

I tossed the ball to Rodney and he walked it up the court for the final shot. He called for me to come set a pick, but then changed his mind.

I floated back down underneath the basket, stepping in and out of the paint to avoid a three second violation. The reserves were playing off of everyone but Rodney to prevent him from driving to the basket. With ten seconds to go, he gave me a look. He didn't say anything, it was just a look, and I knew exactly what he wanted me to do. I ran up to set a screen for him on the left side, but instead of rolling to the open space, I slipped toward the hoop. Rodney fit a perfect pass in to me through the smallest of cracks in the defense, and by the time I gathered the ball, took one dribble, and laid the ball in the basket off the glass, there was no time left. The buzzer sounded and the scrimmage was over. It was my first game-winning shot. I was never a good enough offensive player to be able to take the last shot in the game.

"That's what I'm talkin' about!" Rodney yelled.

We jumped up and bumped chests hard. I smiled—a real smile.

Coach came over and gave me a hard pat on the back.

"That's how you turn it around," he said. "With toughness."

———

I met a lot of my teammates' parents during the party after practice. I could see in their eyes and hear in their voices the pride that they had in their sons for reaching this level in sports. Seeing the families interact with each other brought on a bit of sadness to me because my family was not there to celebrate. I wondered, if my dad were still alive, would he be proud of me just like the other dads? There was no way to know that.

Towards the end of the party, my teammates and their parents went off into small groups to their own little areas of the gym and talked amongst themselves.

I slipped out of the gym unnoticed and into the

locker room. I quickly showered and changed before leaving school. I waited a few minutes outside the front entrance for the bus to come, and when it did, I got on and found a seat in the back. My legs were thankful for the rest; the heavy weight on my shoulders was still there.

FIFTEEN

I was exhausted by the time I got off the bus in front of Miss Grace's apartment. I needed to close my eyes. I needed to rest. It was getting dark out, though. Halstead was busy with people walking up and down on both sides. There wasn't any trouble. I looked out for it constantly after that night at the corner store.

I passed by some men standing in front of the entrance to my building. I had seen them before and they recognized me too. We exchanged nods as I passed by them. One of them shouted, "sup nigga." I nodded and headed into the building. I wondered, is this what it felt like to be an American?

When I got upstairs, no one was home. As usual, Miss Grace left a note for me telling me that there was food and how to prepare it. I wasn't hungry, though. I had a little food at the party before and still didn't have much of an appetite. I went into my room and closed the door. The window was cracked and I closed it as well. I wanted the room to get warm. I remembered the warmth in Darfur, and that it would sometimes help me sleep.

My eyes were heavy as I got under the blanket. I pulled it over my face and left a little hole to breathe through. Sleep came fast.

—

My father was sitting at the table. He didn't say any-thing to me. He just smiled and looked on. I looked around the room for my brother Sefu, but he wasn't there. There was loud noise coming from outside the window, but I didn't feel afraid. At first, I couldn't say what the noise was. And even after I figured it out, it didn't matter. I knew that my father would protect me.

I tried to get close to him. I wanted to give him a hug. But it was impossible. When I tried to touch him, my hand would just go through him like he was a ghost, like he was invisible.

A wind blew into the room and mixed with the noise from outside. I wanted to talk to my father one last time. The wind came so strong that it blew the door open. I could see their shadows right outside the door. They were coming closer and closer. I looked back to my father and he wasn't there anymore. He was gone. Something told me that it would be this way forever. That it was always going to hurt and that I was just going to have to understand.

The shadows got closer to the door, but I didn't back away from them.

The phone rang and I woke up with a gasp. It was Kyle on the other end.

"Kyle?"

"Serge," he said. "How have you been?"

I ignored this question. "Where have you been?" I asked. "I haven't seen you at school."

"That day in the park made me think, Serge. Well, first it made me sad. Then it made me think."

"I have something to tell you, Kyle."

"Go ahead."

"My father and brother were killed in Sudan," I blurted out. "Shot by rebels."

Kyle didn't say anything. But I could hear his breathing get heavier on the other end of the line.

"The shooting I witnessed at the corner store brought up a lot of bad memories," I said.

"It's hard to let those things go," he said.

"Yes. It is."

"Do you think you ever will?" he asked.

"I don't know."

There was silence for a little while.

"Well, anyway, the reason I called was to tell you that I'm leaving school," he said. "I'm leaving Chicago."

"What?" I asked. "You love it here. Where will you go?"

"There is a family back in Kenya. Our two families were close when my parents were still alive. I'm going to live with them and go to my old school there."

"You're going back to Kenya? Why would you want to go back there?" I asked "The place where your parents were killed?"

"I don't know; it just feels right. Being here, alone in America, just doesn't feel right anymore. I'm not sure it ever did."

"Are you sure?"

"Yeah," he said. "You think I'm crazy for going back there?"

"Crazy?" I said. "No. You're just looking for something."

"Yeah."

"Well, I guess this is goodbye then," I said.

"Bye, Serge."

"Bye Kyle," I said. "Thanks again for helping me out."

"It's nothing," he said. "Oh, Serge. If you ever feel any guilt—and I'm just saying this because I felt guilty after my parents were killed, guilty that I got to keep living and they didn't—if those feelings ever come, just know that they'll go away."

I took a deep breath.

"I'll do that, Kyle."

I hung up the phone and got out of bed. I opened the window and stuck my head out. The night was calm and the cold air burned my chest as I took deep breaths. There were no sirens, no people standing outside, and the cars that did drive by had their windows rolled up. The silence was not empty, though. It's just that it was too cold out. The streets were cold.

I closed the window and sat down in bed. I thought about my first day in Chicago, my first day at school, and the first time I went to Grant Park with Kyle. Those were moments that were filled with both excitement and anxiety. I didn't know what to expect during my time in Chicago and that was just fine. I was learning how to deal with the feelings I had from the past, but not ready to let them go.

Kyle had his own journey to make back to Africa. I hoped that he could find the peace he was searching for. It would be hard losing a friend—my only one—but it was clear that going back to Kenya was something he had to do.

I was thankful that he called me to say goodbye. That was actually the first time I had ever received a telephone call from a friend. Something told me that this wouldn't be the last time I saw Kyle in Chicago. He loved the city. I could see it in his eyes. It would be a perfect ending for him to go to Kenya and find his peace only to come back home again. This time, though, he wouldn't be alone when he got back. He'd have a friend waiting here for him, a friend from Sudan that he could talk with about the pain.

My eyes got heavier as I fought off sleep. I was so used to not sleeping because of the nightmares that it felt like I needed to learn how do to it all over again. Something inside me told me that it was okay, though, that I could put my head down and rest.

By the time I got back into to bed it was late. I closed my eyes hoping there wouldn't be any nightmares. There were many things I wanted at that moment, but a peaceful sleep would've been good enough.

I woke up on Sunday morning to the smell of Miss Grace's cooking. Miss Grace, Mike, and I had breakfast together—a meal of bacon and eggs. Things felt normal again, like they did before the corner store incident. Mike read his newspaper like he did every Sunday, leaving Miss Grace and I responsible for the conversation. There was a rhythm to life and I was getting used to it.

"You're feeling better, aren't you?" she asked.

I nodded. "I am."

"I can tell."

She smiled.

"Can I ask you a question, Miss Grace?"

"Sure."

"When is it okay to let something go from your past?"

"That's not an easy one," she said.

"Is it okay if I never let it go?"

"I know they say that holding on to the past can stop you from looking toward the future," she said. "But you have to make that choice. Nobody can *tell* you how to feel, Serge."

After breakfast, I went to my room to organize it. I gathered all of my school and workout clothes to take down to the Laundromat. I didn't even empty my clothes sack when I first arrived because of school and basketball. I took the clothes that were inside of the sack and placed them in the dresser drawers. I reached down to the bottom of the clothes sack and pulled out a large, folded sheet of paper. When I unfolded it, a smaller piece of paper dropped to the floor. The larger piece was a picture of my entire family. I remembered the day we took that picture. It was one of the last days that we were all together. I was standing next to my father and Sefu because that's the way it always was. I bent down to pick up the small sheet of paper from the floor. It was a note from my mother. I recognized her handwriting instantly and the familiarity sent a shot of warmth throughout my body. I read the note once. Then read it again. I couldn't believe that I had overlooked it.

The note began with my mother saying that she thought that she could express herself best through a note. And that she was proud of me for leaving Sudan in hopes of creating a better life for myself.

She thought that the strength I showed in leaving would help me get through the difficulties in life. She didn't see a future for me in Sudan—a future that didn't end with a bullet, anyway.

But what the note said next was new to me. It was about my father and Sefu and *why* they were killed. I didn't know many details about the night that they were killed or of what led to it. I just knew that the rebels were coming around more and more arguing with my father about something. I was caught up in my own life, too focused on basketball to notice what was happening with my own family. The men that killed my father and Sefu were members of the Janjaweed. They wanted me to join their militia to help them with their efforts in the genocide. They wanted me because of my physical stature and competitive streak. To say that the Janjaweed *wanted* me to join, though, would have been incorrect. They *demanded* that I join their ranks. My father, though, would not allow it.

Then it all made sense: the night of their deaths, my father sending me out into the woods. My mother didn't say it in the note; she didn't say that my father and Sefu died so that I could make it out of Sudan alive. That's what it was, though, and that was the way that I chose to remember it.

I folded the note and put it in one of the drawers of my desk. I hadn't talked to my mother since I left and really wasn't sure where her and my siblings were living. Wherever they were, I hoped that they were safe. A shot of guilt—the kind that Kyle talked to me about on the phone—rushed through my body. Here I was in America, going to school, playing a game, and my mother and siblings were stuck in Sudan living on the run. But I had to let go of it. This note from my mother was a gift. I no longer believed that my father thought I was a disgrace. He just didn't know what to do with a son who was good at playing basketball. He didn't know how to react when his son fell in love with a game. He didn't know how to protect me—to protect my gift. Suddenly, I realized what was at stake for me. My father and brother had died to protect me. There was no greater honor.

The nightmares never came back again.

SIXTEEN

On the morning of the first game of the season, I got to school early to go see Coach in his office. He wasn't expecting me, but I knew he'd be there. I had a lot of energy; the anticipation of the first game of the season was felt through every hallway in school. Anywhere you looked, there were banners and signs from classmates wishing the team luck for not only the first game, but also the whole season. As I walked through the gym on the way to Coach's office, I stopped at midcourt to think about where I had come from. It was empty inside the gym, and silent. My dream was still a young one—one that didn't even exist five years before.

I felt at peace there on the court, like always. I closed my eyes, took a deep breath, and knew that if I had the strength to make it here from Sudan, playing the game with everything I had would be easy. *Are you strong enough, Serge?* Yes. Yes I am, because my family is in my heart—and I chase my dreams for them.

I opened my eyes and looked around the gym one final time. I walked off the floor to the locker room, and then to Coach's office.

I found him there at his desk and he looked up at me with surprise when I entered his doorway.

"Serge."

"Hey Coach."

"You're early."

"I think I'm excited for the first game. You know, my first game in America."

"I am, too."

I stood there silent for a moment.

"Everything okay?" he asked.

"I just, I've been thinking a lot lately and talking

to a lot of people. I said. "And I finally realized that I have something to play for other than myself. I've found my purpose."

"Tell me."

"I will make it all the way to the NBA so that I can bring my family to America," I said. "That's my duty to my family."

He smiled.

"That sounds great, Serge," he said. "I'll be here to help you any way I can. You can do it."

Playing the game and playing hard would be my tribute to my family, to the memory of my father and Sefu, to my country, and finally, to myself. I was going to make something out of my life, either through basketball or school, or maybe both. I wasn't going to let my mother down and wasn't going to give up until my family was with me in America.

There were still a couple of hours before the game and the only other person in the locker room was Rodney. Things mattered to him. Basketball mattered. Being nice to me when no one else on the team would be mattered to him. I felt a connection to Rodney on the court from the first time I stepped out there with him. Even though we came from different places, basketball had its own language that brought us closer. We both had a focus. A purpose.

I wanted to know people like Rodney. I wanted to be around people who cared about things.

Kyle was the same. We had a unique bond based on an unlikely, yet shared past; a past shaped by loss.

I sat down in front of my locker and nodded to Rodney as he was sitting listening to music.

"What's up, Serge?" he asked, bobbing his head up and down. I could hear the music blaring out of his headphones.

"Not much," I said. "You?"

He pulled his headphones off of his head.

"Chillin'," he said. "You'll see a whole different version of me, though, when that ball gets tossed up in the air tonight."

"Yeah, I'm looking forward to it, too," I said.

"You've come a long way from that first day in the weight room."

We both had a smile about that.

"Thanks again for having my back, Rodney."

"Ah man, it ain't no thing," he said. "The guys get you now. They know what you're about. Playing hard, playing tough, and winning."

We were silent for a little while after that. He put his headphones back into his ears and I pulled out the next novel that I had to read for English class. The story was written by an African writer who had fled the continent and come to America to find opportunity and success.

I was interested in the book, but my excitement for the first game of the season left me stuck on the first sentence. It was no use. There would be plenty of time to read; it was time to play. I thought about it all: my father, the clerk, Kyle's parents, Sudan. I couldn't help but smile. Through it all, I was still here, and I had many people to thank for that.

I looked over to Rodney and nodded at him again.

He took his headphones out and mouthed, "What's up?"

"Nothing," I said. "It's just that when you come from where I come, it's hard to enjoy the journey."

"I know what you mean," he said. "I come from South Side. The hood, you feel me?"

"Yes, I do. I wish this game would hurry up and come," I said. "I can't wait anymore."

"Just wait on it, Serge," he said. "Trust me. It'll be sweeter if you wait on it."